C0-ATA-845

OTHER ANTHOLOGIES BY TERRY CARR

The Best Science Fiction of the Year
New Worlds of Fantasy
New Worlds of Fantasy #2
New Worlds of Fantasy #3
On Our Way to the Future
The Others
Science Fiction for People Who Hate Science Fiction
This Side of Infinity
Universe 1
Universe 2

WITH DONALD A. WOLLHEIM

World's Best Science Fiction: 1965–1971 (7 volumes)

AN EXALTATION OF STARS

Transcendental Adventures in Science Fiction

COMPILED AND EDITED BY

TERRY CARR

SIMON AND SCHUSTER · NEW YORK

Published by Simon and Schuster
Rockefeller Center, 630 Fifth Avenue
New York, New York 10020

First printing

SBN 671-21469-1
Library of Congress Catalog Card Number: 72-89253
Designed by Edith Fowler
Manufactured in the United States of America

CONTENTS

INTRODUCTION

Science fiction is a literature of rationality. In its "pure" form, in stories based solidly on logical extrapolation of known scientific principles, it is the most rigorously rational form of literature we've ever had.

Yet, seemingly paradoxically, science fiction has always been fascinated by the irrational, the numinous and transcendental. I suppose this is because science fiction likes to ask large questions: not simply *How?* but *Why?* And what are the implications? So we've had novels such as James Blish's *A Case of Conscience,* Michael Moorcock's *Behold the Man,* Walter M. Miller, Jr.'s *A Canticle for Leibowitz.* Even so purely a "hard-science-fiction" writer as Arthur C. Clarke has long been fascinated by the possibilities of transcendental experience . . . readers of his early novel *Childhood's End* could not have been too surprised that 2001 ended as it did.

Science fiction concerns itself, ultimately, with cosmology. Explicitly or implicitly, the questions at the core of most serious SF stories have to do with the nature of our entire reality, the reaches of the universe . . . and what this means for mankind. Origins are as important to the scientific mind as to the religious one, though for different reasons: the religious man's interest in the beginning is really a question about the end: what is our Purpose, why are we here? whereas the rationalist asks about beginnings because he wants to learn about his possibilities—he searches for his limits, the limits of his universe, and hopes to find none.

For this book I asked three of SF's most thoughtful writers to effect a blending of the science-fiction genre with questions of transcendental experience. Each responded with a story outside the everyday mode of science fiction, yet each story in its own way remains true to SF's greater traditions. Aside from the additional creative spark that seems to have gone into these stories, you may find as I did that the methods by which these three authors reconciled and joined the rational and the irrational are impressive and rewarding.

Robert Silverberg, in *The Feast of St. Dionysus,* tells of an astronaut returned alone and guilt-ridden from Mars, his mates dead on that other world; and with careful delineation of thought and emotion Silverberg shows us one man's way out of his own dark night toward a Light.

Roger Zelazny's novella considers the forms spiritual ecstasy might take not only for a man, but for an entirely different form of life. His conclusions are thought-provoking, and all the more so for being embodied in a story of such a pragmatic thing as murder.

Edgar Pangborn returns us to human religion in *My Brother Leopold,* but he addresses not the transcendental experience alone, but its effects and implications. Here, in a future post-holocaust North America whose civilization is only now rebuilding itself out of dark ages, we meet a man who has felt the Presence, and we see the results of his attempt to relate a higher knowledge to earthly reality.

Three very different approaches, and three sharply contrasting stories. But you may find it most rewarding to consider the similarities that run through them: these stories aren't about the gathering of mere data, but rather of experience; they offer not pat answers, but well-formulated questions. And their focus is always, as it should be, on human beings: what might religion come to mean to us under new circumstances?

The questions are rational, the experiences aren't. Isn't that how it happens in life?

TERRY CARR

Oakland, California

THE FEAST OF ST. DIONYSUS

Robert Silverberg

Sleepers, awake. Sleep is separateness; the cave of solitude is the cave of dreams, the cave of the passive spectator. To be awake is to participate, carnally and not in fantasy, in the feast; the great communion.

—Norman O. Brown: *Love's Body*

This is the dawn of the day of the Feast. Oxenshuer knows roughly what to expect, for he has spied on the children at their catechisms, he has had hints from some of the adults, he has spoken at length with the high priest of this strange apocalyptic city; and yet, for all his patiently gathered knowledge, he really knows nothing at all of today's event. What will happen? They will come for him: Matt, who has been appointed his brother, and Will and Nick, who are his sponsors. They will lead him through the labyrinth to the place of the saint, to the god-house at the city's core. They will give him wine until he is glutted, until his cheeks and chin drip with it and his robe is stained with red. And he and Matt will struggle, will have a contest of some sort, a wrestling match, an agon: whether real or symbolic, he does not yet know. Before the whole community they will contend. What else, what else? There will be hymns to the saint, to the god—god and saint, both are one, Dionysus and Jesus, each an aspect of the other. Each a manifestation of the divinity we carry within us, so the Speaker has said. Jesus and Dionysus, Dionysus and Jesus, god and saint, saint and god, what do the terms matter? He has heard the people singing:

This is the god who burns like fire
This is the god whose name is music
This is the god whose soul is wine

Fire. Music. Wine. The healing fire, the joining fire, in which all things will be made one. By its leaping blaze he will drink and drink and drink, dance and dance and dance. Maybe there will be some sort of sexual event—an orgy perhaps, for sex and religion are closely bound among these people: a communion of the flesh opening the way toward communality of spirit.

I go to the god's house and his fire consumes me
I cry the god's name and his thunder deafens me
I take the god's cup and his wine dissolves me

And then? And then? How can he possibly know what will happen, until it has happened? "You will enter into the ocean of Christ," they have told him. An ocean? Here in the Mojave Desert? Well, a figurative ocean, a metaphorical ocean. All is metaphor here. "Dionysus will carry you to Jesus," they say. Go, child, swim out to God. Jesus waits. The saint, the mad saint, the boozy old god who is their saint, the mad saintly god who abolishes walls and makes all things one, will lead you to bliss, dear John, dear tired John. Give your soul gladly to Dionysus the Saint. Make yourself whole in his blessed fire.

You've been divided too long. How can you lie dead on Mars and still walk alive on Earth?

Heal yourself, John. This is the day.

From Los Angeles the old San Bernardino Freeway rolls eastward through the plastic suburbs, through Alhambra and Azusa, past the Covina Hills branch of Forest Lawn Memorial Parks, past the mushroom sprawl of San Bernardino, which is becoming a little Los Angeles, but not so little. The highway pushes onward into the desert like a flat gray cincture holding the dry brown hills asunder. This was the road by which John Oxenshuer finally chose to make his escape. He had had no particular destination in mind but was seeking only a parched place, a sandy place, a place where he could be alone: he needed to re-create, in what might well be his last weeks of life, certain aspects of barren Mars. After considering a number of possibilities he fastened upon this route, attracted to it by the way the freeway seemed to lose itself in the desert north of the Salton Sea. Even in this overcivilized epoch a man could easily disappear there.

Late one November afternoon, two weeks past his fortieth birthday, he closed his rented apartment on Hollywood Boulevard. Taking leave of no one, he drove unhurriedly toward the freeway entrance. There he surrendered control to the electronic highway net, which seized his car and pulled it into the traffic flow. The net governed him as far as Covina; when he saw Forest Lawn's statuary-speckled hilltop coming up on his right, he readied himself to resume driving. A mile beyond the vast cemetery a blinking sign told him he was on his own, and he took the wheel. The car continued to slice inland at the same mechanical velocity of 140 kilometers per hour. With each moment the recent past dropped from him, bit by bit.

Can you drown in the desert? Let's give it a try, God. I'll make a bargain with You. You let me drown out there. All right? And I'll give myself to You. Let me sink into the sand, let me bathe in it, let it wash Mars out of my soul, let it drown me, God, let it drown me. Free me from Mars and I'm yours, God. Is it a deal? Drown me in the desert and I'll surrender at last. I'll surrender.

At twilight he was in Banning. Some gesture of farewell to civilization seemed suddenly appropriate, and he risked stopping to have dinner at a small Mexican restaurant. It was crowded with families enjoying a night out, which made Oxenshuer fear he would be recognized. Look, someone would cry, there's the Mars astronaut, there's the one who came back! But of course no one spotted him. He had grown a bushy, sandy moustache that nearly obliterated his thin, tense lips. His body, lean and wide-shouldered, no longer had an astronaut's springy erectness; in the nineteen months since his return from the red planet he had begun to stoop a little, to cultivate a roundedness of the upper back, as if some leaden weight beneath his breastbone were tugging him forward and downward. Besides, spacemen are quickly forgotten. How long had anyone remembered the names of the heroic lunar teams of his youth? Borman, Lovell, and Anders. Armstrong, Aldrin, and Collins. Scott, Irwin, and Worden. Each of them had had a few gaudy weeks of fame, and then they had disappeared into the blurred pages of the almanac—all, perhaps, except Armstrong; children learned about him at school. His one small step: he would become a figure of myth, up there with Columbus and Magellan. But the others? Forgotten. Yes. Yesterday's heroes. Oxenshuer, Richardson, and Vogel. Who? Oxenshuer, Richardson, and Vogel. That's Oxenshuer right over there, eating tamales and enchiladas, drinking a bottle of Double-X. He's the one who came back. Had some sort of breakdown and left his wife. Yes. That's a funny name, Oxenshuer. Yes. He's the one who came back. What about the other two? They died. Where did they die, Daddy? They died on Mars, but Oxenshuer came back. What were their names again? Richardson and Vogel. They died. Oh. On Mars. Oh. And Oxenshuer didn't. What were their names again?

Unrecognized, safely forgotten, Oxenshuer finished his meal and returned to the freeway. Night had come by this time. The moon was nearly full; the mountains, clearly outlined against the darkness, glistened with a coppery sheen. There is no moonlight on Mars except the feeble, hasty glow of Phobos, dancing in and out of eclipse on its nervous journey from west to east. He had found Phobos disturbing; nor had he cared for fluttery Deimos, starlike, a tiny rocketing point of light. Oxenshuer drove onward, leaving the zone of urban sprawl behind, entering the true desert, pockmarked here and there by resort towns: Palm Springs, Twentynine Palms, Desert Hot Springs. Beckoning billboards summoned him to the torpid pleasures of whirlpool baths and saunas. These temptations he ignored without difficulty. Dryness was what he sought.

Once he was east of Indio he began looking for a place to abandon the car; but he was still too close to the southern boundaries of Joshua Tree National Monument, and he did not want to make camp this near to any area that might be patrolled by park rangers. So he kept driving until the moon was high and he was deep into the Chuckwalla country, with nothing much except sand dunes and mountains and dry lakebeds between him and the Arizona border. In a stretch where the land seemed relatively flat he slowed the car almost to an idle, killed his lights, and swerved gently off the road, following a vague northeasterly course; he gripped the wheel tightly as he jounced over the rough, crunchy terrain. Half a kilometer from the highway Oxenshuer came to a shallow sloping basin, the dry bed of some ancient lake. He eased down into it until he could no longer see the long yellow tracks of headlights on the road, and knew he must be below the line of sight of any passing vehicle. After turning off the engine, he locked the car—a strange prissiness here, in the midst of nowhere!—took his backpack from the trunk, slipped his arms through the shoulder straps, and, without looking back, began to walk into the emptiness that lay to the north.

As he walked he composed a letter he would never send. *Dear Claire, I wish I had been able to say goodbye to you before I left Los Angeles. I regretted only that: leaving town without telling you. But I was afraid to call. I draw back from you. You say you hold no grudge against me over Dave's death, you say it couldn't possibly have been my fault, and of course you're right. And yet I don't dare face you, Claire. Why is that? Because I left your husband's body on Mars and the guilt of that is choking me? But a body is only a shell, Claire. Dave's body isn't Dave, and there wasn't anything I could do for Dave. What is it, then, that comes between us? Is it my love, Claire, my guilty love for my friend's widow? Eh? That love is salt in my wounds, that love is sand in my throat, Claire. Claire. Claire. I can never tell you any of this, Claire. I never will. Goodbye. Pray for me. Will you pray?*

His years of grueling NASA training for Mars served him well now. Powered by ancient disciplines, he moved swiftly, feeling no strain even with forty-five pounds on his back. He had no trouble with the uneven footing. The sharp chill in the air did not bother him, though he wore only light clothing—slacks and shirt and a flimsy cotton vest. The solitude, far from oppressing him, was actually a source of energy: a couple of hundred kilometers away in Los Angeles it might be the ninth decade of the twentieth century, but this was a prehistoric realm, timeless, unscarred by man, and his spirit expanded in his self-imposed isolation. Conceivably every footprint he made was the first human touch this land had felt. That gray, pervasive sense of guilt, heavy on him since his return from Mars, held less weight for him here beyond civilization's edge.

This wasteland was the closest he could come to attaining Mars on Earth. Not really close enough, for too many things broke the illusion: the great gleaming scarred moon, and the succulent terrestrial vegetation, and the tug of Earth's gravity, and the faint white glow on the leftward horizon that he imagined emanated from the cities of the coastal strip. But it was as close to Mars in flavor as he could manage. The Peruvian desert would have been better, only he had no way of getting to Peru.

An approximation. It would suffice.

A trek of at least a dozen kilometers left him still unfatigued, but he decided, shortly after midnight, to settle down for the night. The site he chose was a small level quadrangle bounded on the north and south by spiky, ominous cacti—chollas and prickly pears—and on the east by a maze of scrubby mesquite; to the west, a broad alluvial fan of tumbled pebbles descended from the nearby hills. Moonlight, raking the area sharply, highlighted every contrast of contour: the shadows of cacti were unfathomable inky pits and the tracks of small animals—lizards and kangaroo rats—were steep-walled canyons in the sand. As he slung his pack to the ground two startled rats, browsing in the mesquite, noticed him belatedly and leaped for cover in wild, desperate bounds, frantic but delicate. Oxenshuer smiled at them.

On the twentieth day of the mission Richardson and Vogel went out, as planned, for the longest extravehicular on the schedule, the ninety-kilometer crawler jaunt to the Gulliver site. "Goddamned well about time," Dave Vogel had muttered when the EVA okay had at last come floating up, time-lagged and crackly, out of far-off Mission Control. All during the eight-month journey from Earth, while the brick-red face of Mars was swelling patiently in their portholes, they had argued about the timing of the big Marswalk—pursuing an argument that had begun six months before launch date. Vogel, insisting that the expedition was the mission's most important scientific project, had wanted to do it first, to get it done and out of the way before mishaps might befall them and force them to scrub it. No matter that the timetable decreed it for Day 20. The timetable was too conservative. "We can overrule Mission Control," Vogel said. "If they don't like it, let them reprimand us when we get home." Bud Richardson, though, wouldn't go along. "Houston knows best," he kept saying. He always took the side of authority. "First we have to get used to working on Mars, Dave. First we ought to do the routine stuff close by the landing site, while we're getting acclimated. What's our hurry? We've got to stay here a month until the return window opens, anyway. Why breach the schedule? The scientists know what they're doing, and they want us to do everything in its proper order," Richardson said. Vogel, stubborn, eager, seething, thought he would find an ally in Oxenshuer. "You vote with me, John. Don't tell me *you* give a crap about Mission Control! Two against one and Bud will have to give in." But Oxenshuer, oddly, took Richardson's side. He hesitated to deviate from the schedule. He wouldn't be making the long extravehicular himself in any case; he had drawn the short straw, he was the man who'd be keeping close to the ship all the time. How then could he vote to alter the carefully designed schedule and send Richardson off, against his will, on a risky and perhaps ill-timed adventure? "No," Oxenshuer said. "Sorry, Dave, it isn't my place to decide such things." Vogel appealed anyway to Mission Control, and Mission Control said, "Wait till Day 20, fellows." On Day 20 Richardson and Vogel suited up and went out. It was the ninth EVA of the mission, but the first that would take anyone more than a couple of kilometers from the ship.

Oxenshuer monitored his departing companions from his safe niche in the control cabin. The small video screen showed him the path of their crawler as it diminished into the somber red plain. You're well named, rusty old Mars. The blood of fallen soldiers stains your soil. Your hills are the color of the flames that lick conquered cities. Jouncing westward across Solis Lacus, Vogel kept up a running commentary. "Lots of dead nothing out here, Johnny. It's as bad as the Moon. A prettier color, though. Are you reading me?" "I'm reading you," Oxenshuer said. The crawler was like a submarine mounted on giant preposterous wheels. Joggle, joggle, joggle, skirting craters and ravines, ridges and scarps. Pausing now and then so Richardson could pop a geological specimen or two into the gunny sack. Then onward, westward, westward. Heading bumpily toward the site where the unmanned Ares IV Mars Lander, almost a decade earlier, had scraped some Martian microorganisms out of the ground with the Gulliver sampling device.

* * *

"Gulliver" is a culture chamber that inoculates itself with a sample of soil. The sample is obtained by two 7½-meter lengths

of kite line wound on small projectiles. When the projectiles are fired, the lines unwind and fall to the ground. A small motor inside the chamber then reels them in, together with adhering soil particles. The chamber contains a growth medium whose organic nutrients are labeled with radioactive carbon. When the medium is inoculated with soil, the accompanying microorganisms metabolize the organic compounds and release radioactive carbon dioxide. This diffuses to the window of a Geiger counter, where the radioactivity is measured. Growth of the microbes causes the rate of carbon dioxide production to increase exponentially with time—an indication that the gas is being formed biologically. Provision is also made for the injection, during the run, of a solution containing a metabolic poison which can be used to confirm the biological origin of the carbon dioxide and to analyze the nature of the metabolic reactions.

* * *

All afternoon the crawler traversed the plain, and the sky deepened from dark purple to utter black, and the untwinkling stars, which on Mars are visible even by day, became more brilliant with the passing hours, and Phobos came streaking by, and then came little hovering Deimos. Oxenshuer, wandering around the ship, took readings on this and that and watched his screen and listened to Dave Vogel's chatter, and Mission Control offered a comment every little while. And during these hours the Martian temperature began its nightly slide down the Centigrade ladder. A thousand kilometers away an inversion of thermal gradients unexpectedly developed, creating fierce currents in the tenuous Martian atmosphere, ripping gouts of red sand loose from the hills, driving wild scarlet clouds eastward toward the Gulliver site. As the sandstorm increased in intensity, the scanner satellites in orbit around Mars detected it and relayed pictures of it to Earth, and after the normal transmission lag it was duly noted at Mission Control as a potential hazard to the men in the crawler; but somehow—the NASA hearings did not succeed in fixing blame for this inexplicable communications failure—no one passed the necessary warning along to the three astronauts on Mars. Two hours after he had finished his solitary dinner aboard the ship, Oxenshuer heard Vogel say,

"Okay, Johnny, we've finally reached the Gulliver site, and as soon as we have our lighting system set up we'll get out and see what the hell we have here." Then the sandstorm struck in full fury. Oxenshuer heard nothing more from either of his companions.

Making camp for the night, he took first from his pack his operations beacon, one of his NASA souvenirs. By the sleek instrument's cool, inexhaustible green light he laid out his bedroll in the flattest, least pebbly place he could find; then, discovering himself far from sleepy, Oxenshuer set about assembling his solar still. Although he had no idea how long he would stay in the desert—a week, a month, a year, forever—he had brought perhaps a month's supply of food concentrates with him, but no water other than a single canteen's worth, to tide him through thirst on this first night. He could not count on finding wells or streams here, any more than he had on Mars, and, unlike the kangaroo rats, capable of living indefinitely on nothing but dried seeds, producing water metabolically by the oxidation of carbohydrates, he would not be able to dispense entirely with fresh water. But the solar still would see him through.

He began to dig.

Methodically he shaped a conical hole a meter in diameter, half a meter deep, and put a wide-mouthed two-liter jug at its deepest point. He collected pieces of cactus, breaking off slabs of prickly pear but ignoring the stiletto-spined chollas, and placed these along the slopes of the hole. Then he lined the hole with a sheet of clear plastic film, weighting it by rocks in such a way that the plastic came in contact with the soil only at the hole's rim and hung suspended a few centimeters above the cactus pieces and the jug. The job took him twenty minutes. Solar energy would do the rest: as sunlight passed through the plastic into the soil and the plant material, water would evaporate, condense in droplets on the underside of the plastic, and trickle into the jug. With cactus as juicy as this, he might be able to count on a liter a day of sweet water out of each hole he dug. The still was emergency gear developed for use on Mars; it hadn't done anyone any good there, but Oxenshuer had no fears of running dry in this far more hospitable desert.

Enough. He shucked his pants and crawled into his sleeping bag. At last he was where he wanted to be: enclosed, protected, yet at the same time alone, unsurrounded, cut off from his past in a world of dryness.

He could not yet sleep; his mind ticked too actively. Images out of the last few years floated insistently through it and had to be purged, one by one. To begin with, his wife's face. (Wife? I have no wife. Not now.) He was having difficulty remembering Lenore's features, the shape of her nose, the turn of her lips, but a general sense of her existence still burdened him. How long had they been married? Eleven years, was it? Twelve? The anniversary? March 30, 31? He was sure he had loved her once. What had happened? Why had he recoiled from her touch?

——No, please, don't do that. I don't want to yet.

——You've been home three months, John.

Her sad green eyes. Her tender smile. A stranger, now. His ex-wife's face turned to mist and the mist congealed into the face of Claire Vogel. A sharper image: dark glittering eyes, the narrow mouth, thin cheeks framed by loose streamers of unbound black hair. The widow Vogel, dignified in her grief, trying to console him.

——I'm sorry, Claire. They just disappeared, is all. There wasn't anything I could do.

——John, John, it wasn't your fault. Don't let it get you like this.

——I couldn't even find the bodies. I wanted to look for them, but it was all sand everywhere—sand, dust, the craters, confusion; no signal, no landmarks—no way, Claire, no way.

——It's all right, John. What do the bodies matter? You did your best. I know you did.

Her words offered comfort but no absolution from guilt. Her embrace—light, chaste—merely troubled him. The pressure of her heavy breasts against him made him tremble. He remembered Dave Vogel, halfway to Mars, speaking lovingly of Claire's breasts. Her jugs, he called them. "Boy, I'd like to have my hands on my lady's jugs right this minute!" And Bud Richardson, more annoyed than amused, telling him to cut it out, to stop stirring up fantasies that couldn't be satisfied for another year or more.

Claire vanished from his mind, driven out by a blaze of flashbulbs. The hovercameras, hanging in midair, scanning him from every angle. The taut, earnest faces of the newsmen, digging deep for human interest. See the lone survivor of the Mars expedition! See his tortured eyes! See his gaunt cheeks! "There's the President himself, folks, giving John Oxenshuer a great big welcome back to Earth! What thoughts must be going through this man's mind, the only human being to walk the sands of an alien world and return to our old down-to-Earth planet! How keenly he must feel the tragedy of the two lost astronauts he left behind up there! There he goes now, there goes John Oxenshuer, disappearing into the debriefing chamber—"

Yes, the debriefings. Colonel Schmidt, Dr. Harkness, Commander Thompson, Dr. Burdette, Dr. Horowitz, milking him for data. Their voices carefully gentle, their manner informal, their eyes all the same betraying their singlemindedness.

——Once again, please, Captain Oxenshuer. You lost the signal, right, and then the backup line refused to check out, you couldn't get any telemetry at all. And then?

——And then I took a directional fix, I did a thermal scan and tripled the infrared, I rigged an extension lifeline to the sample-collector and went outside looking for them. But the collector's range was only ten kilometers. And the dust storm was too much. The dust storm. Too damned much. I went five hundred meters and you ordered me back into the ship. Didn't want to go back, but you ordered me.

——We didn't want to lose you too, John.

——But maybe it wasn't too late, even then. Maybe.

——There was no way you could have reached them in a short-range vehicle.

——I would have figured some way of recharging it. If only you had let me. If only the sand hadn't been flying around like that. If. Only.

——I think we've covered the point fully.

——Yes. May we go over some of the topographical data now, Captain Oxenshuer?

——Please. Please. Some other time.

It was three days before they realized what sort of shape he was in. They still thought he was the old John Oxenshuer, the one who had amused himself during the training period by reversing the inputs on his landing simulator, just for the hell of it, the one who had surreptitiously turned on the unsuspecting Secretary of Defense just before a Houston press conference, the one who had sung bawdy carols at a pious Christmas party for the families of the astronauts in '86. Now, seeing him darkened and turned in on himself, they concluded eventually that he had been transformed by Mars, and they sent him, finally, the chief psychiatric team, Mendelson and McChesney.

——How long have you felt this way, Captain?

——I don't know. Since they died. Since I took off for Earth. Since I entered Earth's atmosphere. I don't know. Maybe it started earlier. Maybe it was always like this.

——What are the usual symptoms of the disturbance?

——Not wanting to see anybody. Not wanting to talk to anybody. Not wanting to be with anybody. Especially myself. I'm so goddamned sick of my own company.

——And what are your plans now?

——Just to live quietly and grope my way back to normal.

——Would you say it was the length of the voyage that upset you most, or the amount of time you had to spend in solitude on the homeward leg, or your distress over the deaths of—

——Look, how would I know?

——Who'd know better?

——Hey, I don't believe in either of you, you know? You're figments. Go away. Vanish.

——We understand you're putting in for retirement and a maximum-disability pension, Captain.

——Where'd you hear that? It's a stinking lie. I'm going to be okay before long. I'll be back on active duty before Christmas, you got that?

——Of course, Captain.

——Go. Disappear. Who needs you?

——John, John, it wasn't your fault. Don't let it get you like this.

——I couldn't even find the bodies. I wanted to look for them, but it was all sand everywhere—sand, dust, the craters, confusion; no signal, no landmarks—no way, Claire, no way.

The images were breaking up, dwindling, going. He saw scattered glints of light slowly whirling overhead, the kaleidoscope of the heavens, the whole astronomical psychedelia swaying and cavorting, and then the sky calmed, and then only Claire's face remained, Claire and the minute red disk of Mars. The events of the nineteen months contracted to a single star-bright point of time, and became as nothing, and were gone. Silence and darkness enveloped him. Lying tense and rigid on the desert floor, he stared up defiantly at Mars, and closed his eyes, and wiped the red disk from the screen of his mind, and slowly, gradually, reluctantly, he surrendered himself to sleep.

Voices woke him. Male voices, quiet and deep, discussing him in an indistinct buzz. He hovered a moment on the border between dream and reality, uncertain of his perceptions and unsure of his proper response; then his military reflexes took over and he snapped into instant wakefulness, blinking his eyes open, sitting up in one quick move, rising to a standing position in the next, poising his body to defend itself.

He took stock. Sunrise was maybe half an hour away; the tips of the mountains to the west were stained with early pinkness. Thin mist shrouded the low-lying land. Three men stood just beyond the place where he had mounted his beacon. The shortest one was as tall as he, and they were desert-tanned, heavyset, strong and capable-looking. They wore their hair long and their beards full; they were oddly dressed, shepherd-style, in loose belted robes of light green muslin or linen. Although their expressions were open and friendly and they did not seem to be armed, Oxenshuer was troubled by awareness of his vulnerability in this emptiness, and he found menace in their presence. Their intrusion on his isolation angered him. He stared at them warily, rocking on the balls of his feet.

One, bigger than the others, a massive, thick-cheeked, blue-eyed man, said, "Easy. Easy, now. You look all ready to fight."

"Who are you? What do you want?"

"Just came to find out if you were okay. You lost?"

Oxenshuer indicated his neat camp, his backpack, his bedroll. "Do I seem lost?"

"You're a long way from anywhere," said the man closest to Oxenshuer, one with shaggy yellow hair and a cast in one eye.

"Am I? I thought it was just a short hike from the road."

The three men began to laugh. "You don't know *where* the hell you are, do you?" said the squint-eyed one. And the third one, dark-bearded, hawk-featured, said, "Look over thataway." He pointed behind Oxenshuer, to the north. Slowly, half anticipating trickery, Oxenshuer turned. Last night, in the moonlit darkness, the land had seemed level and empty in that direction, but now he beheld two steeply rising mesas a few hundred meters apart, and in the opening between them he saw a low wooden palisade, and behind the palisade the flat-roofed tops of buildings were visible, tinted orange-pink by the spreading touch of dawn. A settlement out here? But the map showed nothing, and, from the looks of it, that was a town of some two or three thousand people. He wondered if he had somehow been transported by magic during the night to some deeper part of the desert. But no: there was his solar still, there was the mesquite patch, there were last night's prickly pears. Frowning, Oxenshuer said, "What is that place in there?"

"The City of the Word of God," said the hawk-faced one calmly.

"You're lucky," said the squint-eyed one. "You've been brought to us almost in time for the Feast of Saint Dionysus. When all men are made one. When every ill is healed."

Oxenshuer understood. Religious fanatics. A secret retreat in the desert. The state was full of apocalyptic cults, more and more of them now that the end of the century was only about ten years away and millenary fears were mounting. He scowled. He had a native Easterner's innate distaste for Californian irrationality. Reaching into the reservoir of his own decaying Catholicism, he said thinly, "Don't you mean Saint *Dionysius*? With an *i*? Dionysus was the Greek god of wine."

"Dionysus," said the big blue-eyed man. "Dionysius is somebody else, some Frenchman. We've heard of him. Dionysus is who we mean." He put forth his hand. "My name's Matt, Mr. Oxenshuer. If you stay for the Feast, I'll stand brother to you. How's that?"

The sound of his name jolted him. "You've heard of me?"

"Heard of you? Well, not exactly. We looked in your wallet."

"We ought to go now," said the squint-eyed one. "Don't want to miss breakfast."

"Thanks," Oxenshuer said, "but I think I'll pass up the invitation. I came out here to get away from people for a little while."

"So did we," Matt said.

"You've been called," said Squint-eye hoarsely. "Don't you realize that, man? You've been called to our city. It wasn't any accident you came here."

"No?"

"There aren't any accidents," said Hawk-face. "Not ever. Not in the breast of Jesus, not ever a one. What's written is written. You were called, Mr. Oxenshuer. Can you say no?" He put his hand lightly on Oxenshuer's arm. "Come to our city. Come to the Feast. Look, why do you want to be afraid?"

"I'm not afraid. I'm just looking to be alone."

"We'll let you be alone, if that's what you want," Hawk-face told him. "Won't we, Matt? Won't we, Will? But you can't say no to our city. To our saint. To Jesus. Come along, now. Will, you carry his pack. Let him walk into the city without a burden." Hawk-face's sharp, forbidding features were softened by the glow of his fervor. His dark eyes gleamed. A strange, persuasive warmth leaped from him to Oxenshuer. "You won't say no. You won't. Come sing with us. Come to the Feast. Well?"

"Well?" Matt asked also.

"To lay down your burden," said squint-eyed Will. "To join the singing. Well? Well?"

"I'll go with you," Oxenshuer said at length. "But I'll carry my own pack."

They moved to one side and waited in silence while he assembled his belongings. In ten minutes everything was in order. Kneeling, adjusting the straps of his pack, he nodded and looked up. The early sun was full on the city now, and its rooftops were bright with a golden radiance. Light seemed to stream upward from them; the entire desert appeared to blaze in that luminous flow.

"All right," Oxenshuer said, rising and shouldering his pack. "Let's go." But he remained where he stood, staring ahead. He felt the city's golden luminosity as a fiery tangible force on his cheeks, like the outpouring of heat from a crucible of molten metal. With Matt leading the way the three men walked ahead, single file, moving fast. Will, the squint-eyed one, bringing up the rear, paused to look back questioningly at Oxenshuer, who was still standing entranced by the sight of that supernal brilliance. "Coming," Oxenshuer murmured. Matching the pace of the others, he followed them briskly over the parched, sandy wastes toward the City of the Word of God.

There are places in the coastal desert of Peru where no rainfall has ever been recorded. On the Paracas Peninsula, about eleven miles south of the port of Pisco, the red sand is absolutely bare of all vegetation: not a leaf, not a living thing; no stream enters the ocean nearby. The nearest human habitation is several miles away where wells tap underground water and a few sedges line the beach. There is no more arid area in the western hemisphere; it is the epitome of loneliness and desolation. The psychological landscape of Paracas is much the same as that of Mars. John Oxenshuer, Dave Vogel, and Bud Richardson spent three weeks camping there in the winter of 1987, testing their emergency gear and familiarizing themselves with the emotional texture of the Martian environment. Beneath the sands of the peninsula are found the desiccated bodies of an ancient people unknown to history, together with some of the most magnificent textiles that the world has ever seen. Natives seeking salable artifacts have rifled the necropolis of Paracas, and now the bones of its occupants lie scattered on the surface, and the winds alternately cover and uncover fragments of the coarser fabrics, discarded by the diggers, still soft and strong after nearly two millennia.

Vultures circle high over the Mojave. They would pick the bones of anyone who had died here. There are no vultures on Mars. Dead men become mummies, not skeletons, for nothing decays on Mars. What has died on Mars remains buried in the sand, invulnerable to time, imperishable, eternal. Perhaps archaeologists, bound on a futile but inevitable search for the remains of the lost races of old Mars, will find the withered bodies of Dave Vogel and Bud Richardson in a mound of red soil, ten thousand years from now.

At close range the city seemed less magical. It was laid out in the form of a bull's-eye, its curving streets set in concentric rings behind the blunt-topped little palisade, evidently purely symbolic in purpose, that rimmed its circumference between the mesas. The buildings were squat stucco affairs of five or six rooms, unpretentious and undistinguished, all of them similar if not identical in style: pastel-hued structures of the sort found everywhere in southern California. They seemed to be twenty or thirty years old and in generally shabby condition; they were set close together and close to the street, with no gardens and no garages. Wide avenues leading inward pierced the rings of buildings every few hundred meters. This seemed to be entirely a residential district, but no people were in sight, either at windows or on the streets, nor were there any parked cars; it was like a movie set, clean and empty and artificial. Oxenshuer's footfalls echoed loudly. The silence and surreal emptiness troubled him. Only an occasional child's tricycle, casually abandoned outside a house, gave evidence of recent human presence.

As they approached the core of the city, Oxenshuer saw that the avenues were narrowing and then giving way to a labyrinthine tangle of smaller streets, as intricate a maze as could be found in any of the old towns of Europe; the bewildering pattern seemed deliberate and carefully designed, perhaps for the sake of shielding the central section and making it a place apart from the antiseptic, prosaic zone of houses in the outer rings. The buildings lining the streets of the maze had an institutional character: they were three and four stories high, built of red brick, with few windows and pinched, unwelcoming entrances. They had the look of nineteenth-century hotels; possibly they were warehouses and meeting halls and places of some municipal nature. All were deserted. No commercial establishments were visible—no shops, no restaurants, no banks, no loan companies, no theaters, no newsstands. Such things were forbidden, maybe, in a theocracy such as Oxenshuer suspected this place to be. The city plainly had not evolved in any helter-skelter free-enterprise fashion, but had been planned down to its last alleyway for the exclusive use of a communal order whose members were beyond the bourgeois needs of an ordinary town.

Matt led them surefootedly into the maze, infallibly choosing connecting points that carried them steadily deeper toward the center. He twisted and turned abruptly through juncture after juncture, never once doubling back on his track. At last they stepped through one passageway barely wide enough for Oxenshuer's pack, and he found himself in a plaza of unexpected size and grandeur. It was a vast open space, roomy enough for several thousand people, paved with cobbles that glittered in the harsh desert sunlight. On the right was a colossal building two stories high that ran the entire length of the plaza, at least three hundred meters; it looked as bleak as a barracks, a dreary utilitarian thing of clapboard and aluminum siding painted a dingy drab green, but all down its plaza side were tall, radiant stained-glass windows, as incongruous as pink gardenias blooming on a scrub oak. A towering metal cross rising high over the middle of the pointed roof settled all doubts: this was the city's church. Facing it across the plaza was an equally immense building, no less unsightly, built to the same plan but evidently secular, for its windows were plain and it bore no cross. At the far side of the plaza, opposite the place where they had entered it, stood a much smaller structure of dark stone in an implausible Gothic style, all vaults and turrets and arches. Pointing to each building in turn, Matt said, "Over there's the house of the god. On this side's the dining hall. Straight ahead, the little one, that's the house of the Speaker. You'll meet him at breakfast. Let's go eat."

. . . Captain Oxenshuer and Major Vogel, who will spend the next year and a half together in the sardine-can environment of their spaceship as they make their round-trip journey to Mars and back, are no strangers to each other. Born on the same day —November 4, 1949—in Reading, Pennsylvania, they grew up together, attending the same elementary and high schools as classmates and sharing a dormitory room as undergraduates at Princeton. They dated many of the same girls; it was Captain Oxenshuer who introduced Major Vogel to his future wife, the former Claire Barnes, in 1973. "You might say he stole her from me," the tall, slender astronaut likes to tell interviewers, grinning to show he holds no malice over the incident. In a sense Major Vogel returned the compliment, for Captain Oxenshuer has been married since March 30, 1978, to the major's first cousin, the former Lenore Reiser, whom he met at his friend's wedding reception. After receiving advanced scientific degrees—Captain Oxenshuer in meteorology and celestial mechanics, Major Vogel in geology and space navigation—they enrolled together in the space program in the spring of 1979 and shortly afterward were chosen as members of the original 36-man group of trainees for the first manned flight to the red planet. According to their fellow astronauts, they quickly distinguished themselves for their fast and imaginative responses to stress situations, for their extraordinarily deft teamwork, and also for their shared love of high-spirited pranks and gags, which got them into trouble more than once with sober-sided NASA officials. Despite occasional reprimands, they were regarded as obvious choices for the initial Mars voyage, for which their selection was announced on March 18, 1985. Colonel Walter ("Bud") Richardson, named that day as command pilot for the Mars mis-

sion, cannot claim to share the lifelong bonds of companionship that link Captain Oxenshuer and Major Vogel, but he has been closely associated with them in the astronaut program for the past ten years and long ago established himself as their most intimate friend. Colonel Richardson, the third of this country's three musketeers of interplanetary exploration, was born in Omaha, Nebraska, on the 5th of June, 1948. He hoped to become an astronaut from earliest childhood onward, and . . .

They crossed the plaza to the dining hall. Just within the entrance was a dark-walled low-ceilinged vestibule; a pair of swinging doors gave access to the dining rooms beyond. Through windows set in the doors Oxenshuer could glimpse dimly lit vastnesses to the left and the right, in which great numbers of solemn people, all clad in the same sort of flowing robes as his three companions, sat at long bare wooden tables and passed serving bowls around. Nick told Oxenshuer to drop his pack and leave it in the vestibule; no one would bother it, he said. As they started to go in, a boy of ten erupted explosively out of the left-hand doorway, nearly colliding with Oxenshuer. The boy halted just barely in time, backed up a couple of paces, stared with shameless curiosity into Oxenshuer's face, and, grinning broadly, pointed to Oxenshuer's bare chin and stroked his own as if to indicate that it was odd to see a man without a beard. Matt caught the boy by the shoulders and pulled him against his chest; Oxenshuer thought he was going to shake him, to chastise him for such irreverence, but no, Matt gave the boy an affectionate hug, swung him far overhead, and tenderly set him down. The boy clasped Matt's powerful forearms briefly and went sprinting through the right-hand door.

"Your son?" Oxenshuer asked.

"Nephew. I've got two hundred nephews. Every man in this town's my brother, right? So every boy's my nephew."

——If I could have just a few moments for one or two questions, Captain Oxenshuer.

——Provided it's really just a few moments. I'm due at Mission Control at O-eight-thirty, and—

——I'll confine myself, then, to the one topic of greatest relevance to our readers. What are your feelings about the Deity, Captain? Do you, as an astronaut soon to depart for Mars, believe in the existence of God?

——My biographical poop sheet will tell you that I've been known to go to Mass now and then.

——Yes, of course, we realize you're a practicing member of the Catholic faith, but, well, Captain, it's widely understood that for some astronauts religious observance is more of a public-relations matter than a matter of genuine spiritual urgings. Meaning no offense, Captain, we're trying to ascertain the actual nature of your relationship, if any, to the Divine Presence, rather than—

——All right. You're asking a complicated question and I don't see how I can give an easy answer. If you're asking whether I literally believe in the Father, Son, and Holy Ghost, whether I think Jesus came down from heaven for our salvation and was crucified for us and was buried and on the third day rose again and ascended into heaven, I'd have to say no. Not except in the loosest metaphorical sense. But I do believe —ah—suppose we say I believe in the existence of an organizing force in the universe, a power of sublime reason that makes everything hang together, an underlying principle of rightness. Which we can call God for lack of a better name. And which I reach toward, when I feel I need to, by way of the Roman Church, because that's how I was raised.

——That's an extremely abstract philosophy, Captain.

——Abstract. Yes.

——That's an extremely rationalistic approach. Would you say that your brand of cool rationalism is characteristic of the entire astronaut group?

——I can't speak for the whole group. We didn't come out of a single mold. We've got some all-American boys who go to church every Sunday and think that God himself is listening in person to every word they say, and we've got a couple of atheists, though I won't tell you who, and we've got guys who just don't care one way or the other. And I can tell you we've got a few real mystics, too, some out-and-out guru types. Don't let the uniforms and haircuts fool you. Why, there are times when I feel the pull of mysticism myself.

——In what way?

——I'm not sure. I get a sense of being on the edge of some sort of cosmic breakthrough. An awareness that there may be real forces just beyond my reach, not abstractions but actual functioning dynamic entities, which I could attune myself to if I only knew how to find the key. You feel stuff like that when you go into space, no matter how much of a rationalist you think you are. I've felt it four or five times, on training flights, on orbital missions. I want to feel it again. I want to break through. I want to reach God, am I making myself clear? I want to reach God.

——But you say you don't literally believe in Him, Captain. That sounds contradictory to me.

——Does it really?

——It does, sir.

——Well, if it does, I don't apologize. I don't have to think straight all the time. I'm entitled to a few contradictions. I'm capable of holding a couple of diametrically opposed beliefs. Look, if I want to flirt with madness a little, what's it to you?

——Madness, Captain?

——Madness. Yes. That's exactly what it is, friend. There are times when Johnny Oxenshuer is tired of being so goddamned sane. You can quote me on that. Did you get it straight? There are times when Johnny Oxenshuer is tired of being so goddamned sane. But don't print it until I've blasted off for Mars, you hear me? I don't want to get bumped from this mission for incipient schizophrenia. I want to go. Maybe I'll find God out there this time, you know? And maybe I won't. But I want to go.

——I think I understand what you're saying, sir. God bless you, Captain Oxenshuer. A safe voyage to you.

——Sure. Thanks. Was I of any help?

Hardly anyone glanced up at him, only a few of the children, as Matt led him down the long aisle toward the table on the platform at the back of the hall. The people here appeared to be extraordinarily self-contained, as if they were in possession of some wondrous secret from which he would be forever excluded, and the passing of the serving bowls seemed far more interesting to them than the stranger in their midst. The smell of scrambled eggs dominated the great room. That heavy greasy odor seemed to expand and rise until it squeezed out all the air. Oxenshuer found himself choking and gagging. Panic seized him. He had never imagined he could be thrown into terror by the smell of scrambled eggs. "This way," Matt called. "Steady on, man. You all right?" Finally they reached the raised table. Here sat only men, dignified and serene of mien, probably the elders of the community. At the head of the table was one who had the unmistakable look of a high priest. He was well past seventy—or eighty or ninety—and his strong-featured leathery face was seamed and gullied; his eyes were keen and intense, managing to convey both a fierce tenacity and an all-encompassing warm humanity. Small-bodied, lithe, weighing at most one hundred pounds, he sat ferociously erect, a formidably commanding little man. A metallic embellishment of the collar of his robe was, perhaps, the badge of his status. Leaning over him, Matt said in exaggeratedly clear, loud tones, "This here's John. I'd like to stand brother to him when the Feast comes, if I can. John, this here's our Speaker."

Oxenshuer had met popes and presidents and secretaries-general, and, armored by his own standing as a celebrity, had never fallen into foolish awe-kindled embarrassment. But here he was no celebrity, he was no one at all, a stranger, an outsider, and he found himself lost before the Speaker. Mute, he waited for help. The old man said, his voice as melodious and as resonant as a cello, "Will you join our meal, John? Be welcome in our city."

Two of the elders made room on the bench. Oxenshuer sat at the Speaker's left hand; Matt sat beside him. Two girls of about fourteen brought settings: a plastic dish, a knife, a fork, a spoon, a cup. Matt served him: scrambled eggs, toast, sausages. All about him the clamor of eating went on. The Speaker's plate was empty. Oxenshuer fought back nausea and forced himself to attack the eggs. "We take all our meals together," said the Speaker. "This is a closely knit community, unlike any community I know on Earth." One of the serving girls said pleasantly, "Excuse me, brother" and, reaching over Oxenshuer's shoulder, filled his cup with red wine. Wine for breakfast? They worship Dionysus here, Oxenshuer remembered.

The Speaker said, "We'll house you. We'll feed you. We'll love you. We'll lead you to God. That's why you're here, isn't it? To get closer to Him, eh? To enter into the ocean of Christ."

——What do you want to be when you grow up, Johnny?

——An astronaut, ma'am. I want to be the first man to fly to Mars.

No. He had never said any such thing.

Later in the morning he moved into Matt's house, on the perimeter of the city, overlooking one of the mesas. The house was merely a small green box, clapboard outside, flimsy beaverboard partitions inside: a sitting room, three bedrooms, a bathroom. No kitchen or dining room. ("We take all our meals together.") The walls were bare: no ikons, no crucifixes, no religious paraphernalia of any kind. No television, no radio, hardly any personal possessions at all in evidence: a dozen worn books and magazines, some spare robes and extra boots in a closet, little more than that. Matt's wife was a small, quiet woman in her late thirties, soft-eyed, submissive, dwarfed by her burly husband. Her name was Jean. There were three children, a boy of about twelve and two girls, maybe nine and seven. The boy had had a room of his own; he moved uncomplainingly in with his sisters, who doubled up in one bed to provide one for him, and Oxenshuer took the boy's room. Matt told the children their guest's name, but it drew no response from them. Obviously they had never heard of him. Were they even aware that a spaceship from Earth had lately journeyed to Mars? Probably not. He found that refreshing: for years Oxenshuer had had to cope with children paralyzed with astonishment at finding themselves in the presence of a genuine astronaut. Here he could shed the burdens of fame.

He realized he had not been told his host's last name. Somehow it seemed too late to ask Matt directly, now. When one of the little girls came wandering into his room he asked her, "What's your name?"

"Toby," she said, showing a gap-toothed mouth.

"Toby what?"

"Toby. Just Toby."

No surnames in this community? All right. Why bother with surnames in a place where everyone knows everyone else? Travel light, brethren, travel light, strip away the excess baggage.

Matt walked in and said, "At council tonight I'll officially apply to stand brother to you. It's just a formality. They've never turned an application down."

"What's involved, actually?"

"It's hard to explain until you know our ways better. It means I'm, well, your spokesman, your guide through our rituals."

"A kind of sponsor?"

"Well, sponsor's the wrong word. Will and Nick will be your sponsors. That's a different level of brotherhood, lower, not as close. I'll be something like your godfather, I guess, that's as near as I can come to the idea. Unless you don't want me to be. I never consulted you. Do you want me to stand brother to you, John?"

It was an impossible question. Oxenshuer had no way to evaluate any of this. Feeling dishonest, he said, "It would be a great honor, Matt."

"You have any real brothers?" Matt asked. "Flesh kin?"

"No. A sister in Ohio." Oxenshuer thought a moment. "There once was a man who was like a brother to me. Knew him since childhood. As close as makes no difference. A brother, yes."

"What happened to him?"

"He died. In an accident. A long way from here."

"Terrible sorry," Matt said. "I've got five brothers. Three of them outside; I haven't heard from them in years. And two right here in the city. You'll meet them. They'll accept you as kin. Everyone will. What did you think of the Speaker?"

"A marvelous old man. I'd like to talk with him again."

"You'll talk plenty with him. He's my father, you know."

Oxenshuer tried to imagine this huge man springing from the

seed of the spare-bodied, compactly built Speaker and could not make the connection. He decided Matt must be speaking metaphorically again. "You mean, the way that boy was your nephew?"

"He's my true father," Matt said. "I'm flesh of his flesh." He went to the window. It was open about eight centimeters at the bottom. "Too cold for you in here, John?"

"It's fine."

"Gets cold sometimes, these winter nights."

Matt stood silent, seemingly sizing Oxenshuer up. Then he said, "Say, you ever do any wrestling?"

"A little. In college."

"That's good."

"Why do you ask?"

"One of the things brothers do here, part of the ritual. We wrestle some. Especially the day of the Feast. It's important in the worship. I wouldn't want to hurt you any when we do. You and me, John, we'll do some wrestling before long, just to practice up for the Feast, okay? Okay?"

They let him go anywhere he pleased. Alone, he wandered through the city's labyrinth, that incredible tangle of downtown streets, in early afternoon. The maze was cunningly constructed, one street winding into another so marvelously that the buildings were drawn tightly together and the bright desert sun could barely penetrate; Oxenshuer walked in shadow much of the way. The twisting mazy passages baffled him. The purpose of this part of the city seemed clearly symbolic: everyone who dwelt here was compelled to pass through these coiling, interlacing streets in order to get from the commonplace residential quarter, where people lived in isolated family groupings, to the dining hall, where the entire community together took the sacrament of food, and to the church, where redemption and salvation were to be had. Only when purged of error and doubt, only when familiar with the one true way (or was there more than one way through the maze? Oxenshuer wondered) could one attain the harmony of communality. He was still uninitiated, an outlander; wander as he would, dance tirelessly from street to cloistered street, he would never get there unaided.

He thought it would be less difficult than it had first seemed to find his way from Matt's house to the inner plaza, but he was wrong: the narrow, meandering streets misled him, so that he sometimes moved away from the plaza when he thought he was going toward it, and, after pursuing one series of corridors and intersections for fifteen minutes, he realized that he had merely returned himself to one of the residential streets on the edge of the maze. Intently he tried again. An astronaut trained to maneuver safely through the trackless wastes of Mars ought to be able to get about in one small city. Watch for landmarks, Johnny. Follow the pattern of the shadows. He clamped his lips, concentrated, plotted a course. As he prowled he occasionally saw faces peering briefly at him out of the upper windows of the austere warehouselike buildings that flanked the streets. Were they smiling? He came to one group of streets that seemed familiar to him, and went in and in, until he entered an alleyway closed at both ends, from which the only exit was a slit barely wide enough for a man if he held his breath and slipped through sideways. Just beyond, the metal cross of the church stood outlined against the sky, encouraging him: he was nearly to the end of the maze. He went through the slit and found himself in a cul-de-sac; five minutes of close inspection revealed no way to go on. He retraced his steps and sought another route.

One of the bigger buildings in the labyrinth was evidently a school. He could hear the high, clear voices of children chanting mysterious hymns. The melodies were conventional seesaws of piety, but the words were strange:

Bring us together. Lead us to the ocean.
Help us to swim. Give us to drink.
Wine in my heart today,
Blood in my throat today,
Fire in my soul today,
All praise, O God, to thee.

Sweet treble voices, making the bizarre words sound all the more grotesque. Blood in my throat today. Unreal city. How can it exist? Where does the food come from? Where does the wine come from? What do they use for money? What do the people do with themselves all day? They have electricity: what fuel keeps the generator running? They have running water. Are they hooked into a public-utility district's pipelines, and if so why isn't this place on my map? Fire in my soul today. Wine in my heart today. What are these feasts, who are these saints? This is the god who burns like fire. This is the god whose name is music. This is the god whose soul is wine. You were called, Mr. Oxenshuer. Can you say no? You can't say no to our city. To our saint. To Jesus. Come along, now?

Where's the way out of here?

Three times a day, the whole population of the city went on foot from their houses through the labyrinth to the dining hall. There appeared to be at least half a dozen ways of reaching the central plaza, but, though he studied the route carefully each time, Oxenshuer was unable to keep it straight in his mind. The food was simple and nourishing, and there was plenty of it. Wine flowed freely at every meal. Young boys and girls did the serving, jubilantly hauling huge platters of food from the kitchen; Oxenshuer had no idea who did the cooking, but he supposed the task would rotate among the women of the community. (The men had other chores. The city, Oxenshuer learned, had been built entirely by the freely contributed labor of its own inhabitants. Several new houses were under construction now. And there were irrigated fields beyond the mesas.) Seating in the dining hall was random at the long tables, but people generally seemed to come together in nuclear-family groupings. Oxenshuer met Matt's two brothers, Jim and Ernie, both smaller men than Matt but powerfully built. Ernie gave Oxenshuer a hug—a quick, warm, impulsive gesture. "Brother," he said. "Brother! Brother!"

The Speaker received Oxenshuer in the study of his residence on the plaza, a dark ground-floor room whose walls were covered to ceiling height with shelves of books. Most people here affected a casual hayseed manner, an easy, drawling, rural simplicity of speech, that implied little interest in intellectual things, but the Speaker's books ran heavily to abstruse philosophical and theological themes, and they looked as though they had all been read many times. Those books confirmed Oxenshuer's first fragmentary impression of the Speaker: that this was a man of supple, well-stocked mind, sophisticated, complex. The Speaker offered Oxenshuer a cup of cool, tart wine. They drank in silence. When he had nearly drained his cup, the old man calmly hurled the dregs to the glossy slate floor. "An offering to Dionysus," he explained.

"But you're Christians here," said Oxenshuer.

"Yes, of course we're Christian! But we have our own calendar of saints. We worship Jesus in the guise of Dionysus and Dionysus in the guise of Jesus. Others might call us pagans, I suppose. But where there's Christ, is there not Christianity?" The Speaker laughed. "Are you a Christian, John?"

"I suppose. I was baptized. I was confirmed. I've taken communion. I've been to confession now and then."

"You're of the Roman faith?"

"More that faith than any other," Oxenshuer said.

"You believe in God?"

"In an abstract way."

"And in Jesus Christ?"

"I don't know," said Oxenshuer uncomfortably. "In a literal sense, no. I mean, I suppose there was a prophet in Palestine named Jesus, and the Romans nailed him up, but I've never taken the rest of the story too seriously. I can accept Jesus as a symbol, though. As a metaphor of love. God's love."

"A metaphor for *all* love," the Speaker said. "The love of God for mankind. The love of mankind for God. The love of man and woman, the love of parent and child, the love of brother and brother, every kind of love there is. Jesus is love's spirit. God is love. That's what we believe here. Through communal ecstasies we are reminded of the new commandment He gave unto us, That ye love one another. And as it says in Romans, Love is the fulfilling of the law. We follow His teachings; therefore we are Christians."

"Even though you worship Dionysus as a saint?"

"Especially so. We believe that in the divine madnesses of Dionysus we come closer to Him than other Christians are capable of coming. Through revelry, through singing, through the pleasures of the flesh, through ecstasy, through union with one another in body and in soul—through these we break out of our isolation and become one with Him. In the life to come we shall all be one. But first we must live this life and share in the creation of love, which is Jesus, which is God. Our goal is to make all beings one with Jesus, so that we become droplets in the ocean of love which is God, giving up our individual selves."

"This sounds Hindu to me, almost. Or Buddhist."

"Jesus is Buddha. Buddha is Jesus."

"Neither of them taught a religion of revelry."

"Dionysus did. We make our own synthesis of spiritual commandments. And so we see no virtue in self-denial, since that is the contradiction of love. What is held to be virtue by other Christians is sin to us. And vice versa, I would suppose."

"What about the doctrine of the virgin birth? What about the virginity of Jesus himself? The whole notion of purity through restraint and asceticism?"

"Those concepts are not part of our belief, friend John."

"But you do recognize the concept of sin?"

"The sins we deplore," said the Speaker, "are such things as coldness, selfishness, aloofness, envy, maliciousness, all those things that hold one man apart from another. We punish the sinful by engulfing them in love. But we recognize no sins that arise out of love itself or out of excess of love. Since the world, especially the Christian world, finds our principles hateful and dangerous, we have chosen to withdraw from that world."

"How long have you been out here?" Oxenshuer asked.

"Many years. No one bothers us. Few strangers come to us. You are the first in a very long time."

"Why did you have me brought to your city?"

"We knew you were sent to us," the Speaker said.

At night there were wild, frenzied gatherings in certain tall, windowless buildings in the depths of the labyrinth. He was never allowed to take part. The dancing, the singing, the drinking, whatever else went on, these things were not yet for him. Wait till the Feast, they told him, wait till the Feast, then you'll be invited to join us. So he spent his evenings alone. Some nights he would stay home with the children. No babysitters were needed in this city, but he became one anyway, playing simple dice games with the girls, tossing a ball back and forth with the boy, telling them stories as they fell asleep. He told them of his flight to Mars, spoke of watching the red world grow larger every day, described the landing, the alien feel of the place, the iron-red sands, the tiny glinting moons. They listened silently, perhaps fascinated, perhaps not at all interested: he suspected they thought he was making it all up. He never said anything about the fate of his companions.

Some nights he would stroll through town, street after quiet street, drifting in what he pretended was a random way toward the downtown maze. Standing near the perimeter of the labyrinth—even now he could not find his way around in it after dark, and feared getting lost if he went in too deep—he would listen to the distant sounds of the celebration, the drumming, the chanting, the simple, repetitive hymns:

This is the god who burns like fire
This is the god whose name is music
This is the god whose soul is wine

And he would also hear them sing:

Tell the saint to heat my heart
Tell the saint to give me breath
Tell the saint to quench my thirst

And this:

Leaping shouting singing stamping
Rising climbing flying soaring
Melting joining loving blazing
Singing soaring joining loving

Some nights he would walk to the edge of the desert, hiking out a few hundred meters into it, drawing a bleak pleasure from the solitude, the crunch of sand beneath his boots, the knife-blade coldness of the air, the forlorn gnarled cacti, the timorous kangaroo rats, even the occasional scorpion. Crouching on some gritty hummock, looking up through the cold brilliant stars to the red dot of Mars, he would think of Dave Vogel, would think of Bud Richardson, would think of Claire, and of himself, who he had been, what he had lost. Once, he remembered, he had been a high-spirited man who laughed easily, expressed affection readily and openly, enjoyed joking, drinking, running, swimming—all the active, outgoing things. Leaping shouting singing stamping. Rising climbing flying soaring. And then this deadness had come over him, this zombie absence of response, this icy shell. Mars had stolen him from himself. Why? The guilt? The guilt, the guilt, the guilt—he had lost himself in guilt. And now he was lost in the desert. This implausible town. These rites, this cult. Wine and shouting. He had no idea how long he had been here. Was Christmas approaching? Possibly it was only a few days away. Blue plastic Yule trees were sprouting in front of the department stores on Wilshire Boulevard. Jolly red Santas pacing the sidewalk. Tinsel and glitter. Christmas might be an appropriate time for the Feast of St. Dionysus. The Saturnalia revived. Would the Feast come soon? He anticipated it with fear and eagerness.

Late in the evening, when the last of the wine was gone and the singing was over, Matt and Jean would return, flushed, wine-drenched, happy, and through the thin partition separating Oxenshuer's room from theirs would come the sounds of love, the titanic poundings of their embraces, far into the night.

——Astronauts are supposed to be sane, Dave.
——Are they? Are they really, Johnny?
——Of course they are.
——Are *you* sane?
——I'm sane as hell, Dave.
——Yes. Yes. I'll bet you think you are.

——Don't you think I'm sane?

——Oh, sure, you're sane, Johnny. Saner than you need to be. If anybody asked me to name him one sane man, I'd say John Oxenshuer. But you're not all that sane. And you've got the potential to become very crazy.

——Thanks.

——I mean it as a compliment.

——What about you? You aren't sane?

——I'm a madman, Johnny. And getting madder all the time.

——Suppose NASA finds out that Dave Vogel's a madman?

——They won't, my friend. They know I'm one hell of an astronaut, and so by definition I'm sane. They don't know what's inside me. They can't. By definition, they wouldn't be NASA bureaucrats if they could tell what's inside a man.

——They know you're sane because you're an astronaut?

——Of course, Johnny. What does an astronaut know about the irrational? What sort of capacity for ecstasy does he have, anyway? He trains for ten years, he jogs in a centrifuge, he drills with computers, he runs a thousand simulations before he dares to sneeze, he thinks in spaceman jargon, he goes to church on Sundays and doesn't pray, he turns himself into a machine so he can run the damnedest machines anybody ever thought up. And to outsiders he looks deader than a banker, deader than a stockbroker, deader than a sales manager. Look at him, with his 1975 haircut and his 1965 uniform. Can a man like that even know what a mystic experience *is*? Well, some of us are really like that. They fit the official astronaut image. Sometimes I think you do, Johnny, or at least that you want to. But not me. Look, I'm a yogi. Yogis train for decades so they can have a glimpse of the All. They subject their bodies to crazy disciplines. They learn highly specialized techniques. A yogi and an astronaut aren't all that far apart, man. What I do, it's not so different from what a yogi does, and it's for the same reason. It's so we can catch sight of the White Light. Look at you, laughing! But I mean it, Johnny. When that big fist knocks me into orbit, when I see the whole world hanging out there, it's a wild moment for me, it's ecstasy, it's nirvana. I live for those moments. They make all the NASA crap worthwhile. Those are breakthrough moments, when I get into an entirely new realm. That's the only reason I'm in this. And you know something? I think it's the same with you, whether you know it or not. A mystic thing, Johnny, a crazy thing, that powers us, that drives us on. The yoga of space. One day you'll find out. One day you'll see yourself for the madman you really are. You'll open up to all the wild forces inside you, the lunatic drives that sent you to NASA. You'll find out you weren't just a machine after all, you weren't just a stockbroker in a fancy costume, you'll find out you're a yogi, a holy man, an ecstatic. And you'll see what a trip you're on, you'll see that controlled madness is the only true secret and that you've always known the Way. And you'll set aside everything that's left of your old straight self. You'll give yourself up completely to forces you can't understand and don't want to understand. And you'll love it, Johnny. You'll love it.

When he had stayed in the city about three weeks—it seemed to him that it had been about three weeks, though perhaps it had been two or four—he decided to leave. The decision was nothing that came upon him suddenly; it had always been in the back of his mind that he did not want to be here, and gradually that feeling came to dominate him. Nick had promised him solitude while he was in the city, if he wanted it, and indeed he had had solitude enough—no one bothering him, no one making demands on him, the city functioning perfectly well without any contribution from him. But it was the wrong kind of solitude. To be alone in the midst of several thousand people was worse than camping by himself in the desert. True, Matt had promised him that after the Feast he would no longer be alone. Yet Oxenshuer wondered if he really wanted to stay there long enough to experience the mysteries of the Feast and the oneness that presumably would follow it. The Speaker spoke of giving up all pain as one enters the all-encompassing body of Jesus. What would he actually give up, though—his pain or his identity? Could he lose one without losing the other? Perhaps it was best to avoid all that and return to his original plan of going off by himself in the wilderness.

One evening after Matt and Jean had set out for the downtown revels, Oxenshuer quietly took his pack from the closet. He checked all his gear, filled his canteen, and said good night to the children. They looked at him strangely, as if wondering why he was putting on his pack just to go for a walk, but they asked no questions. He went up the broad avenue toward the palisade, passed through the unlocked gate, and in ten minutes was in the desert, moving steadily away from the City of the Word of God.

It was a cold, clear night, very dark, the stars almost painfully bright, Mars very much in evidence. He walked roughly eastward, through choppy countryside badly cut by ravines, and soon the mesas that flanked the city were out of sight. He had hoped to cover eight or ten kilometers before making camp, but the ravines made the hike hard going; when he had been out no more than an hour, one of his boots began to chafe him and a muscle in his left leg sprang a cramp. He decided he would do well to halt. He picked a campsite near a stray patch of Joshua trees that stood like grotesque sentinels, stiff-armed and bristly, along the rim of a deep gully. The wind rose suddenly and swept across the desert flats, agitating their angular branches violently. It seemed to Oxenshuer that those booming gusts were blowing him the sounds of singing from the nearby city:

I go to the god's house and his fire consumes me
I cry the god's name and his thunder deafens me
I take the god's cup and his wine dissolves me

He thought of Matt and Jean, and Ernie who had called him brother, and the Speaker who had offered him love and shelter, and Nick and Will, his sponsors. He retraced in his mind the windings of the labyrinth until he grew dizzy. It was impossible, he told himself, to hear the singing from this place. He was at least three or four kilometers away. He prepared his campsite and unrolled his sleeping bag. But it was too early for sleep; he lay wide awake, listening to the wind, counting the stars, playing back the chants of the city in his head. Occasionally he dozed, but only for fitful intervals, easily broken. Tomorrow, he thought, he would cover twenty-five or thirty kilometers, going almost to the foothills of the mountains to the east, and he would set up half a dozen solar stills and settle down for a leisurely reexamination of all that had befallen him.

The hours slipped by slowly. About three in the morning he decided he was not going to be able to sleep, and he got up, dressed, paced along the gully's edge. A sound came to him: soft, almost a throbbing purr. He saw a light in the distance. A second light. The sound redoubled, one purr overlaid by another. Then a third light, farther away. All three lights in motion. He recognized the purring sounds now: the engines of dune cycles. Travelers crossing the desert in the middle of the night? The headlights of the cycles swung in wide circular orbits around him. A search party from the city? Why else would they be driving like that, cutting off arcs of desert in so systematic a way?

Yes. Voices. "John? Jo-ohn! Yo, John!"

Looking for him. But the desert was immense; the searchers were still far off. He need only take his gear and hunker down in the gully, and they would pass him by.

"Yo, John! Jo-ohn!"

Matt's voice.

Oxenshuer walked down the slope of the gully, paused a moment in its depths, and, surprising himself, started to scramble up the gully's far side. There he stood in silence a few minutes, watching the circling dune cycles, listening to the calls of the searchers. It still seemed to him that the wind was bringing him the songs of the city people. This is the god who burns like fire. This is the god whose name is music. Jesus waits. The saint will lead you to bliss, dear tired John. Yes. Yes. At last he cupped his hands to his mouth and shouted, "Yo! Here I am! Yo!"

Two of the cycles halted immediately; the third, swinging out far to the left, stopped a little afterward. Oxenshuer waited for a reply, but none came.

"Yo!" he called again. "Over here, Matt! Here!"

He heard the purring start up. Headlights were in motion once more, the beams traversing the desert and coming to rest on him. The cycles approached. Oxenshuer recrossed the gully, collected his gear, and was waiting again on the cityward side when the searchers reached him. Matt, Nick, Will.

"Spending a night out?" Matt asked. The odor of wine was strong on his breath.

"Guess so."

"We got a little worried when you didn't come back by midnight. Thought you might have stumbled into a dry wash and hurt yourself some. Wasn't any cause for alarm, though, looks like." He glanced at Oxenshuer's pack, but made no comment. "Long as you're all right, I guess we can leave you finish what you were doing. See you in the morning, okay?"

He turned away. Oxenshuer watched the men mount their cycles.

"Wait," he said.

Matt looked around.

"I'm all finished out here," Oxenshuer said. "I'd appreciate a lift back to the city."

"It's a matter of wholeness," the Speaker said. "In the beginning, mankind was all one. We were in contact. The communion of soul to soul. But then it all fell apart. '*In Adam's Fall we sinnéd all,*' remember? And that Fall, that original sin, John, it was a falling apart, a falling away from one another, a falling into the evil of strife. When we were in Eden we were more than simply one family, we were one being, one universal entity; and we came forth from Eden as individuals, Adam and Eve, Cain and Abel. The original universal being broken into pieces. Here, John, we seek to put the pieces back together. Do you follow me?"

"But how is it done?" Oxenshuer asked.

"By allowing Dionysus to lead us to Jesus," the old man said. "And in the saint's holy frenzy to create unity out of opposites. We bring the hostile tribes together. We bring the contending brothers together. We bring man and woman together."

Oxenshuer shrugged. "You talk only in metaphors and parables."

"There's no other way."

"What's your method? What's your underlying principle?"

"Our underlying principle is mystic ecstasy. Our method is to partake of the flesh of the god, and of his blood."

"It sounds very familiar. Take; eat. This is my body. This is my blood. Is your Feast a High Mass?"

The Speaker chuckled. "In a sense. We've made our synthesis between paganism and orthodox Christianity, and we've tried to move backward from the symbolic ritual to the literal act. Do you know where Christianity went astray? The same place all other religions have become derailed. The point at which spiritual experience was replaced by rote worship. Look at your lamas, twirling their prayer wheels. Look at your Jews, muttering about Pharaoh in a language they've forgotten. Look at your Christians, lining up at the communion rail for a wafer and a gulp of wine, and never once feeling the terror and splendor of knowing that they're eating their god! Religion becomes doctrine too soon. It becomes professions of faith, formulas, talismans, emptiness. 'I believe in God the Father Almighty, creator of heaven and earth, and in Jesus Christ his only son, our Lord, who was conceived by the Holy Spirit, born of the Virgin Mary—' Words. Only words. We don't believe, John, that religious worship consists in reciting narrative accounts of ancient history. We want it to be real. We want to *see* our god. We want to *taste* our god. We want to *become* our god."

"How?"

"Do you know anything about the ancient cults of Dionysus?"

"Only that they were wild and bloody, with plenty of drinking and revelry and maybe human sacrifices."

"Yes. Human sacrifices," the Speaker said. "But before the human sacrifices came the divine sacrifices, the god who dies, the god who gives up his life for his people. In the prehistoric Dionysiac cults the god himself was torn apart and eaten; he was the central figure in a mystic rite of destruction in which his ecstatic worshipers feasted on his raw flesh, a sacramental meal enabling them to be made full of the god and take on blessedness, while the dead god became the scapegoat for man's sins.

And then the god was reborn and all things were made one by his rebirth. So in Greece, so in Asia Minor, priests of Dionysus were ripped to pieces as surrogates for the god, and the worshipers partook of blood and meat in cannibalistic feasts of love, and in more civilized times animals were sacrificed in place of men, and still later, when the religion of Jesus replaced the various Dionysiac religions, bread and wine came to serve as the instruments of communion, metaphors for the flesh and blood of the god. On the symbolic level it was all the same. To devour the god. To achieve contact with the god in the most direct way. To experience the rapture of the ecstatic state, when one is possessed by the god. To unite that which society has forced asunder. To break down all boundaries. To rip off all shackles. To yield to our saint, our mad saint, the drunken god who is our saint, the mad saintly god who abolishes walls and makes all things one. Yes, John? We integrate through disintegration. We dissolve in the great ocean. We burn in the great fire. Yes, John? Give your soul gladly to Dionysus the Saint, John. Make yourself whole in his blessed fire. You've been divided too long." The Speaker's eyes had taken on a terrifying gleam. "Yes, John? Yes? Yes?"

In the dining hall one night Oxenshuer drinks much too much wine. The thirst comes upon him gradually and unexpectedly; at the beginning of the meal he simply sips as he eats, in his usual way, but the more he drinks, the more dry his throat becomes, until by the time the meat course is on the table he is reaching compulsively for the carafe every few minutes, filling his cup, draining it, filling, draining, filling, draining. He becomes giddy and boisterous; someone at the table begins a hymn, and Oxenshuer joins in, though he is unsure of the words and keeps losing the melody. Those about him laugh, clap him on the back, sing even louder, beckoning to him, encouraging him to sing with them. Ernie and Matt match him drink for drink, and now whenever his cup is empty they fill it before he has a chance to. A serving girl brings a full carafe. He feels a prickling in his earlobes and the tip of his nose, feels a band of warmth across his chest and shoulders, and realizes he is getting drunk, but he allows it to happen. Dionysus reigns here. He has been sober long enough. And it has occurred to him that his drunkenness perhaps will inspire them to admit him to the night's revels.

But that does not happen. Dinner ends. The Speaker and the other old men who sit at his table file from the hall; it is the signal for the rest to leave. Oxenshuer stands. Falters. Reels. Recovers. Laughs. Links arms with Matt and Ernie. "Brothers," he says. "Brothers!" They go from the hall together, but outside, in the great cobbled plaza, Matt says to him, "You better not go wandering in the desert tonight, man, or you break your neck for sure." So he is still excluded. He goes back through the labyrinth with Matt and Jean to their house, and they help him into his room and give him a jug of wine in case he still feels the thirst, and then they leave him. Oxenshuer sprawls on his bed. His head is spinning. Matt's boy looks in and asks if everything's all right. "Yes," Oxenshuer tells him. "I just need to lie down some." He feels embarrassed over being so helplessly intoxicated, but he reminds himself that in this city of Dionysus no one need apologize for taking too much wine. He closes his eyes and waits for a little stability to return.

In the darkness a vision comes to him: the death of Dave Vogel. With strange brilliant clarity Oxenshuer sees the landscape of Mars spread out on the screen of his mind, low snubby hills sloping down to broad crater-pocked plains, gnarled desolate boulders, purple sky, red gritty particles blowing about. The extravehicular crawler well along on its journey westward toward the Gulliver site, Richardson driving, Vogel busy taking pictures, operating the myriad sensors, leaning into the microphone to describe everything he sees. They are at the Gulliver site now, preparing to leave the crawler, when they are surprised by the sudden onset of the sandstorm. Without warning the sky is red with billowing capes of sand, driving down on them like snowflakes in a blizzard. In the first furious moment of the storm the vehicle is engulfed; within minutes sand is piled a meter high on the crawler's domed transparent roof; they can see nothing, and the sandfall steadily deepens as the storm gains in intensity.

Richardson grabs the controls, but the wheels of the crawler will not grip. "I've never seen anything like this," Vogel mutters. The vehicle has extendible perceptors on stalks, but when Vogel pushes them out to their full reach he finds that they are even then hidden by the sand. The crawler's eyes are blinded; its antennae are buried. They are drowning in sand. Whole dunes are descending on them. "I've never seen anything like this," Vogel says again. "You can't imagine it, Johnny. It hasn't been going on five minutes and we must be under three or four meters of sand already." The crawler's engine strains to free them. "Johnny? I can't hear you, Johnny. Come in, Johnny." All is silent on the ship-to-crawler transmission belt. "Hey, Houston," Vogel says, "we've got this goddamned sandstorm going, and I seem to have lost contact with the ship. Can you raise him for us?" Houston does not reply. "Mission Control, are you reading me?" Vogel asks. He still has some idea of setting up a crawler-to-Earth-to-ship relay, but slowly it occurs to him that he has lost contact with Earth as well. All transmissions have ceased. Sweating suddenly in his spacesuit, Vogel shouts into the microphone, jiggles controls, plugs in the fail-safe communications banks, only to find that everything has failed; sand has invaded the crawler and holds them in a deadly blanket. "Impossible," Richardson says. "Since when is sand an insulator for radio waves?" Vogel shrugs. "It isn't a matter of insulation, dummy. It's a matter of total systems breakdown. I don't know why." They must be ten meters underneath the sand now. Entombed.

Vogel pounds on the hatch, thinking that if they can get out of the crawler somehow they can dig their way to the surface through the loose sand, and then—and then what? Walk back, ninety kilometers, to the ship? Their suits carry thirty-six-hour breathing supplies. They would have to average two and a half kilometers an hour, over ragged cratered country, in order to get there in time; and with this storm raging, their chances of surviving long enough to hike a single kilometer are dismal. Nor does Oxenshuer have a back-up crawler in which he could come out to rescue them, even if he knew their plight; there is only the flimsy little one-man vehicle that they use for short-range geological field trips in the vicinity of the ship.

"You know what?" Vogel says. "We're dead men, Bud." Richardson shakes his head vehemently. "Don't talk garbage. We'll wait out the storm, and then we'll get the hell out of here. Meanwhile we better just pray." There is no conviction in his voice, however. How will they know when the storm is over? Already they lie deep below the new surface of the Martian plain, and everything is snug and tranquil where they are. Tons of sand hold the crawler's hatch shut. There is no escape. Vogel is right: they are dead men. The only remaining question is one of time. Shall they wait for the crawler's air supply to exhaust itself, or shall they take some more immediate step to hasten the inevitable end, going out honorably and quickly and without pain?

Here Oxenshuer's vision falters. He does not know how the trapped men chose to handle the choreography of their deaths. He knows only that whatever their decision was, it must have been reached without bitterness or panic, and that the manner of their departure was calm. The vision fades. He lies alone in the dark. The last of the drunkenness has burned itself from his mind.

"Come on," Matt said. "Let's do some wrestling."

It was a crisp winter morning, not cold, a day of clear hard light. Matt took him downtown, and for the first time Oxenshuer entered one of the tall brick-faced buildings of the labyrinth streets. Inside was a large bare gymnasium, unheated, with bleak yellow walls and threadbare purple mats on the floor. Will and Nick were already there. Their voices echoed in the cavernous room. Quickly Matt stripped down to his undershorts. He looked even bigger naked than clothed; his muscles were thick and rounded, his chest was formidably deep, his thighs were pillars. A dense covering of fair curly hair sprouted everywhere on him, even his back and shoulders. He stood at least two meters tall and must have weighed close to 110 kilos. Oxenshuer, tall but not nearly so tall as Matt, well built but at least twenty kilos lighter, felt himself badly outmatched. He was quick and agile, at any rate: perhaps those qualities would serve him. He tossed his clothing aside.

Matt looked him over closely. "Not bad," he said. "Could use a little more meat on the bones."

"Got to fatten him up some for the Feast, I guess," Will said. He grinned amiably. The three men laughed; the remark seemed less funny to Oxenshuer.

Matt signaled to Nick, who took a flask of wine from a locker and handed it to him. Matt uncorked it, drank deep, and passed the flask to Oxenshuer. It was different from the usual table stuff: thicker, sweeter, almost a sacramental wine. Oxenshuer gulped it down. Then they went to the center mat.

They hunkered into crouches and circled each other tentatively, outstretched arms probing for an opening. Oxenshuer made the first move. He slipped in quickly, finding Matt surprisingly slow on his guard and unsophisticated in defensive technique. Nevertheless, the big man was able to break Oxenshuer's hold with one fierce toss of his body, shaking him off easily and sending him sprawling violently backward. Again they circled. Matt seemed willing to allow Oxenshuer every initiative. Warily Oxenshuer advanced, feinted toward Matt's shoulders, seized an arm instead; but Matt placidly ignored the gambit and somehow pivoted so that Oxenshuer was caught in the momentum of his own onslaught, thrown off balance, vulnerable to a bear hug. Matt forced him to the floor. For thirty seconds or so Oxenshuer stubbornly resisted him, arching his body; then Matt pinned him. They rolled apart and Nick proffered the wine again. Oxenshuer drank, gasping between pulls. "You've got good moves," Matt told him. But he took the second fall even more quickly, and the third with not very much greater effort. "Don't worry," Will murmured to Oxenshuer as they left the gym. "The day of the Feast, the saint will guide you against him."

Every night, now, he drinks heavily, until his face is flushed and his mind is dizzied. Matt, Will, and Nick are always close beside him, seeing to it that his cup never stays dry for long. The wine makes him hazy and groggy, and frequently he has visions as he lies in a stupor on his bed, recovering. He sees Claire Vogel's face glowing in the dark, and the sight of her wrings his heart with love. He engages in long, dreamlike imaginary dialogues with the Speaker on the nature of ecstatic communion. He sees himself dancing in the god-house with the other city folk, dancing himself to exhaustion and ecstasy. He is even visited by St. Dionysus. The saint has a youthful and oddly innocent appearance, with a heavy belly, plump thighs, curling golden hair, a flowing golden beard; he looks like a rejuvenated Santa Claus. "Come," he says softly. "Let's go to the ocean." He takes Oxenshuer's hand and they drift through the silent dark streets, toward the desert, across the swirling dunes, floating in the night, until they reach a broad-bosomed sea, moonlight blazing on its surface like cold white fire. What sea is this? The saint says, "This is the sea that brought you to the world, the undying sea that carries every mortal into life. Why do you ever leave the sea? Here. Step into it with me." Oxenshuer enters. The water is warm, comforting, oddly viscous. He gives himself to it, ankle-deep, shin-deep, thigh-deep; he hears a low murmuring song rising from the gentle waves, and he feels all sorrow going from him, all pain, all sense of himself as a being apart from others. Bathers bob on the breast of the sea. Look: Dave Vogel is here, and Claire, and his parents, and his grandparents, and thousands more whom he does not know; millions, even, a horde stretching far out from shore; all the progeny of Adam, even Adam himself, yes, and Mother Eve, her soft pink body aglow in the water. "Rest," the saint whispers. "Drift. Float. Surrender. Sleep. Give yourself to the ocean, dear John." Oxenshuer asks if he will find God in this ocean. The saint replies, "God *is* the ocean. And God is within you. He always has been. The ocean is God. You are God. I am God. God is everywhere, John, and we are His indivisible atoms. God is everywhere. But before all else, God is within you."

What does the Speaker say? The Speaker speaks Freudian wisdom. Within us all, he says, there dwells a force, an entity—

call it the unconscious; it's as good a name as any—that from its hiding place dominates and controls our lives, though its workings are mysterious and opaque to us. A god within our skulls. We have lost contact with that god, the Speaker says; we are unable to reach it or to comprehend its powers, and so we are divided against ourselves, cut off from the chief source of our strength and cut off, too, from one another: the god that is within me no longer has a way to reach the god that is within you, though you and I both came out of the same primordial ocean, out of that sea of divine unconsciousness in which all being is one. If we could tap that force, the Speaker says, if we could make contact with that hidden god, if we could make it rise into consciousness or allow ourselves to submerge into the realm of unconsciousness, the split in our souls would be healed and we would at last have full access to our godhood. Who knows what kind of creatures we would become then? We would speak, mind to mind. We would travel through space or time, merely by willing it. We would work miracles. The errors of the past could be undone; the patterns of old griefs could be rewoven. We might be able to do anything, the Speaker says, once we have reached that hidden god and transformed ourselves into the gods we were meant to be. Anything. Anything. Anything.

This is the dawn of the day of the Feast. All night long the drums and incantations have resounded through the city. He has been alone in the house, for not even the children were there; everyone was dancing in the plaza, and only he, the uninitiated, remained excluded from the revels. Much of the night he could not sleep. He thought of using wine to lull himself, but he feared the visions the wine might bring, and let the flask be. Now it is early morning, and he must have slept, for he finds himself fluttering up from slumber, but he does not remember having slipped down into it. He sits up. He hears footsteps, someone moving through the house. "John? You awake, John?" Matt's voice. "In here," Oxenshuer calls.

They enter his room: Matt, Will, Nick. Their robes are spotted with splashes of red wine, and their faces are gaunt, eyes red-rimmed and unnaturally bright; plainly they have been up all night. Beneath their fatigue, though, Oxenshuer perceives exhilaration. They are high, very high, almost in an ecstatic state already, and it is only the dawn of the day of the Feast. He sees that their fingers are trembling. Their bodies are tense with expectation.

"We've come for you," Matt says. "Here. Put this on."

He tosses Oxenshuer a robe similar to theirs. All this time Oxenshuer has continued to wear his mundane clothes in the city, making him a marked man, a conspicuous outsider. Naked, he gets out of bed and picks up his undershorts, but Matt shakes his head. Today, he says, only robes are worn. Oxenshuer nods and pulls the robe over his bare body. When he is robed he steps forward; Matt solemnly embraces him, a strong warm hug, and then Will and Nick do the same. The four men leave the house. The long shadows of dawn stretch across the avenue that leads to the labyrinth; the mountains beyond the city are tipped with red. Far ahead, where the avenue gives way to the narrower streets, a tongue of black smoke can be seen licking the sky. The reverberations of the music batter the sides of the buildings. Oxenshuer feels a strange onrush of confidence, and is certain he could negotiate the labyrinth unaided this morning; as they reach its outer border he is actually walking ahead of the others. But sudden confusion confounds him, an inability to distinguish one winding street from another comes over him, and he drops back in silence, allowing Matt to take the lead.

Ten minutes later they reach the plaza.

It presents a crowded, chaotic scene. All the city folk are there, some dancing, some singing, some beating on drums or blowing into trumpets, some lying sprawled in exhaustion. Despite the chill in the air, many robes hang open, and more than a few of the citizens have discarded their clothing entirely. Children run about, squealing and playing tag. Along the front of the dining hall a series of wine barrels has been installed, and the wine gushes freely from the spigots, drenching those who thrust cups forward or simply push their lips to the flow. To the rear, before the house of the Speaker, a wooden platform has sprouted, and the Speaker and the city elders sit enthroned upon it. A gigantic bonfire has been kindled in the center of the plaza, fed by logs from an immense woodpile—hauled no doubt from some storehouse in the labyrinth—that occupies some twenty square meters. The heat of this blaze is tremendous, and it is the smoke from the bonfire that Oxenshuer was able to see from the city's edge.

His arrival in the plaza serves as a signal. Within moments, all is still. The music dies away; the dancing stops; the singers grow quiet; no one moves. Oxenshuer, flanked by his sponsors, Nick and Will, and preceded by his brother, Matt, advances uneasily toward the throne of the Speaker. The old man rises and makes a gesture, evidently a blessing. "Dionysus receive you into His bosom," the Speaker says, his resonant voice traveling far across the plaza. "Drink, and let the saint heal your soul. Drink, and let the holy ocean engulf you. Drink. Drink."

"Drink," Matt says, and guides him toward the barrels. A girl of about fourteen, naked, sweat-shiny, wine-soaked, hands him a cup. Oxenshuer fills it and puts it to his lips. It is the thick sweet wine, the sacramental wine, that he had had on the morning he had practiced wrestling with Matt. It slides easily down his throat; he reaches for more, and then for more when that is gone.

At a signal from the Speaker, the music begins again. The frenzied dancing resumes. Three naked men hurl more logs on the fire and it blazes up ferociously, sending sparks nearly as high as the tip of the cross above the church. Nick and Will and Matt lead Oxenshuer into a circle of dancers who are moving in a whirling, dizzying step around the fire, shouting, chanting, stamping against the cobbles, flinging their arms aloft. At first Oxenshuer is put off by the uninhibited corybantic motions and finds himself self-conscious about imitating them, but as the wine reaches his brain, he sheds all embarrassment and prances with as much gusto as the others: he ceases to be a spectator of himself and becomes fully a participant. Whirl. Stamp. Fling. Shout. Whirl. Stamp. Fling. Shout. The dance centrifuges his mind; pools of blood collect at the walls of his skull and flush the convolutions of his cerebellum as he spins. The heat of the fire makes his skin glow. He sings:

Tell the saint to heat my heart
Tell the saint to give me breath
Tell the saint to quench my thirst

Thirst. When he has been dancing so long that his breath is fire in his throat, he staggers out of the circle and helps himself freely at a spigot. His greed for the thick wine astonishes him. It is as if he has been parched for centuries, every cell of his body shrunken and withered, and only the wine can restore him.

Back to the circle again. His head throbs; his bare feet slap the cobbles; his arms claw the sky. This is the god whose name is music. This is the god whose soul is wine. There are ninety or a hundred people in the central circle of dancers now, and other circles have formed in the corners of the plaza, so that the entire square is a nest of dazzling interlocking vortices of motion. He is being drawn into these vortices, sucked out of himself; he is losing all sense of himself as a discrete individual entity.

Leaping shouting singing stamping
Rising climbing flying soaring
Melting joining loving blazing
Singing soaring joining loving

"Come," Matt murmurs. "It's time for us to do some wrestling."

He discovers that they have constructed a wrestling pit in the far corner of the plaza, over in front of the church. It is square: four low wooden borders, about ten meters long on each side, filled with the coarse sand of the desert. The Speaker has shifted his lofty seat so that he now faces the pit; everyone else is crowded around the place of the wrestling, and all dancing has once again stopped. The crowd opens to admit Matt and Oxenshuer. Not far from the pit Matt shucks his robe; his powerful naked body glistens with sweat. Oxenshuer, after only a moment's hesitation, strips also. They advance toward the entrance of the pit. Before they enter, a boy brings them each a flask of wine. Oxenshuer, already feeling wobbly and hazy from drink, wonders what more wine will do to his physical coordination, but he takes the flask and drinks from it in great gulping swigs. In moments it is empty. A young girl offers him another. "Just take a few sips," Matt advises. "In honor of the god." Oxenshuer does as he is told. Matt is sipping from a second flask too; without warning, Matt grins and flings the contents of his flask over Oxenshuer. Instantly Oxenshuer retaliates. A great cheer goes up; both men are soaked with the sticky red wine. Matt laughs heartily and claps Oxenshuer on the back. They enter the wrestling pit.

Wine in my heart today,
Blood in my throat today,
Fire in my soul today,
All praise, O God, to thee.

They circle each other warily. Brother against brother. Romulus and Remus, Cain and Abel, Osiris and Set: the ancient ritual, the timeless conflict. Neither man offers. Oxenshuer feels heavy with wine, his brain clotted, and yet a strange lightness also possesses him; each time he puts his foot down against the sand the contact gives him a little jolt of ecstasy. He is excitingly aware of being alive, mobile, vigorous. The sensation grows and possesses him, and he rushes forward suddenly, seizes Matt, tries to force him down. They struggle in almost motionless rigidity. Matt will not fall, but his counterthrust is unavailing against Oxenshuer. They stand locked, body against sweat-slick, wine-drenched body, and after perhaps two minutes of intense tension they give up their holds by unvoiced agreement, backing away trembling from each other. They circle again. Brother. Brother. Abel. Cain. Oxenshuer crouches. Extends his hands, groping for a hold. Again they leap toward each other. Again they grapple and freeze. This time Matt's arms pass like bands around Oxenshuer, and he tries to lift Oxenshuer from the ground and hurl him down. Oxenshuer does not budge. Veins swell in Matt's forehead and, Oxenshuer suspects, in his own. Faces grow crimson. Muscles throb with sustained effort. Matt gasps, loosens his grip, tries to step back; instantly Oxenshuer steps to one side of the bigger man, catches his arm, pulls him close. Once more they hug. Each in turn, they sway but do not topple. Wine and exertion blur Oxenshuer's vision; he is intoxicated with strain. Heaving, grabbing, twisting, shoving, he goes round and round the pit with Matt, until abruptly he experiences a dimming of perception, a sharp moment of blackout, and when his senses return to him he is stunned to find himself wrestling not with Matt but with Dave Vogel. Childhood friend, rival in love, comrade in space. Vogel, closer to him than any brother of the flesh, now here in the pit with him: thin sandy hair, snub nose, heavy brows, thick-muscled shoulders. "Dave!" Oxenshuer cries. "Oh, Christ, Dave! Dave!" He throws his arms around the other man. Vogel gives him a mild smile and tumbles to the floor of the pit. "Dave!" Oxenshuer shouts, falling on him. "How did you get here, Dave?" He covers Vogel's body with his own. He embraces him with a terrible grip. He murmurs Vogel's name, whispering in wonder, and lets a thousand questions tumble out. Does Vogel reply? Oxenshuer is not certain. He thinks he hears answers, but they do not match the questions. Then Oxenshuer feels fingers tapping his back. "Okay, John," Will is saying. "You've pinned him fair and square. It's all over. Get up, man."

"Here, I'll give you a hand," says Nick.

In confusion Oxenshuer rises. Matt lies sprawled in the sand, gasping for breath, rubbing the side of his neck, nevertheless still grinning. "That was one hell of a press," Matt says. "That something you learned in college?"

"Do we wrestle another fall now?" Oxenshuer asks.

"No need. We go to the god-house now," Will tells him. They help Matt up. Flasks of wine are brought to them; Oxenshuer gulps greedily. The four of them leave the pit, pass through the opening crowd, and walk toward the church.

Oxenshuer has never been in here before. Except for a sort of altar at the far end, the huge building is wholly empty: no pews, no chairs, no chapels, no pulpit, no choir. A mysterious light filters through the stained-glass windows and suffuses the vast open interior space. The Speaker has already arrived; he stands before the altar. Oxenshuer, at a whispered command from Matt, kneels in front of him. Matt kneels at Oxenshuer's left;

Nick and Will drop down behind them. Organ music, ghostly, ethereal, begins to filter from concealed grillworks. The congregation is assembling; Oxenshuer hears the rustle of people behind him, coughs, some murmuring. The familiar hymns soon echo through the church.

I go to the god's house and his fire consumes me
I cry the god's name and his thunder deafens me
I take the god's cup and his wine dissolves me

Wine. The Speaker offers Oxenshuer a golden chalice. Oxenshuer sips. A different wine: cold, thin. Behind him a new hymn commences, one that he has never heard before, in a language he does not understand. Greek? The rhythms are angular and fierce; this is the music of the Bacchantes, this is an Orphic song, alien and frightening at first, then oddly comforting. Oxenshuer is barely conscious. He comprehends nothing. They are offering him communion. A wafer on a silver dish: dark bread, crisp, incised with an unfamiliar symbol. Take; eat. This is my body. This is my blood. More wine. Figures moving around him, other communicants coming forward. He is losing all sense of time and place. He is departing from the physical dimension and drifting across the breast of an ocean, a great warm sea, a gentle undulating sea that bears him easily and gladly. He is aware of light, warmth, hugeness, weightlessness; but he is aware of nothing tangible. The wine. The wafer. A drug in the wine, perhaps? He slides from the world and into the universe. This is my body. This is my blood. This is the experience of wholeness and unity. I take the god's cup and his wine dissolves me. How calm it is here. How empty. There's no one here, not even me. And everything radiates a pure warm light. I float. I go forth. I. I. I. John Oxenshuer. John Oxenshuer does not exist. John Oxenshuer is the universe. The universe is John Oxenshuer. This is the god whose soul is wine. This is the god whose name is music. This is the god who burns like fire. Sweet flame of oblivion. The cosmos is expanding like a balloon. Growing. Growing. Go, child, swim out to God. Jesus waits.

The saint, the mad saint, the boozy old god who is a saint, will lead you to bliss, dear John. Make yourself whole. Make yourself into nothingness. I go to the god's house and his fire consumes me. Go. Go. Go. I cry the god's name and his thunder deafens me. *Dionysus! Dionysus!*

All things dissolve. All things become one.

This is Mars. Oxenshuer, running his ship on manual, lets it dance lightly down the final five hundred meters to the touchdown site, gently adjusting the yaw and pitch, moving serenely through the swirling red clouds that his rockets are kicking free. Contact light. Engine stop. Engine arm, off.

——All right, Houston, I've landed at Gulliver Base.

His signal streaks across space. Patiently he waits out the lag and gets his reply from Mission Control at last:

——Roger. Are you ready for systems checkout prior to EVA?

——Getting started on it right now, Houston.

He runs through his routines quickly, with the assurance born of total familiarity. All is well aboard the ship; its elegant mechanical brain ticks beautifully and flawlessly. Now Oxenshuer wriggles into his backpack, struggling a little with the cumbersome life-support system; putting it on without any fellow astronauts to help him is more of a chore than he expected, even under the light Martian gravity. He checks out his primary oxygen supply, his ventilating system, his water support loop, his communications system. Helmeted and gloved and fully sealed, he exists now within a totally self-sufficient pocket universe. Unshipping his power shovel, he tests its compressed-air supply. All systems go.

——Do I have a go for cabin depressurization, Houston?

——You are go for cabin depress, John. It's all yours. Go for cabin depress.

He gives the signal and waits for the pressure to bleed down. Dials flutter. At last he can open the hatch. "We have a go for EVA, John." He hoists his power shovel to his shoulder and makes his way carefully down the ladder. Boots bite into red sand. It is midday on Mars in this longitude, and the purple sky has a warm auburn glow. Oxenshuer approaches the burial mound. He is pleased to discover that he has relatively little excavating to do; the force of his rockets during the descent has stripped much of the overburden from his friends' tomb. Swiftly he sets the shovel in place and begins to cut away the remaining sand. Within minutes the glistening dome of the crawler is visible in several places. Now Oxenshuer works more delicately, scraping with care until he has revealed the entire dome. He flashes his light through it and sees the bodies of Vogel and Richardson. They are unhelmeted and their suits are open: casual dress, the best outfit for dying. Vogel sits at the crawler's controls; Richardson lies just behind him on the floor of the vehicle. Their faces are dry, almost fleshless, but their features are still expressive, and Oxenshuer realizes that they must have died peaceful deaths, accepting the end in tranquillity. Patiently he works to lift the crawler's dome. At length the catch yields and the dome swings upward. Oxenshuer climbs in, slips his arms around Dave Vogel's body, and draws it out of the spacesuit. So light: a mummy, an effigy. Vogel seems to have no weight at all. Easily Oxenshuer carries the parched corpse over to the ship. With Vogel in his arms he ascends the ladder. Within, he breaks out the flag-sheathed plastic container NASA has provided and tenderly wraps it around the body. He stows Vogel safely in the ship's hold. Then he returns to the crawler to get Bud Richardson. Within an hour the entire job is done.

——Mission accomplished, Houston.

The landing capsule plummets perfectly into the Pacific. The recovery ship, only three kilometers away, makes for the scene while the helicopters move into position over the bobbing spaceship. Frogmen come forth to secure the flotation collar: the old, old routine. In no time at all the hatch is open. Oxenshuer emerges. The helicopter closest to the capsule lowers its recovery basket; Oxenshuer disappears into the capsule, returning a moment later with Vogel's shrouded body, which he passes across to the swimmers. They load it into the basket and it goes up to the helicopter. Richardson's body follows, and then Oxenshuer himself.

The President is waiting on the deck of the recovery ship. With him are the two widows, black-garbed, dry-eyed, standing straight and firm. The President offers Oxenshuer a warm grin and grips his hand.

——A beautiful job, Captain Oxenshuer. The whole world is grateful to you.

——Thank you, sir.

Oxenshuer embraces the widows. Richardson's wife first: a hug and some soft murmurs of consolation. Then he draws Claire close, conscious of the television cameras. Chastely he squeezes her. Chastely he presses his cheek briefly to hers.

——I had to bring him back, Claire. I couldn't rest until I recovered those bodies.

——You didn't need to, John.

——I did it for you.

He smiles at her. Her eyes are bright and loving.

There is a ceremony on deck. The President bestows posthumous medals on Richardson and Vogel. Oxenshuer wonders whether the medals will be attached to the bodies, like morgue tags, but no, he gives them to the widows. Then Oxenshuer receives a medal for his dramatic return to Mars. The President makes a little speech. Oxenshuer pretends to listen, but his eyes are on Claire more often than not.

With Claire sitting beside him, he sets forth once more out of Los Angeles via the San Bernardino Freeway, eastward through the plastic suburbs, through Alhambra and Azusa, past the Covina Hills Forest Lawn, through San Bernardino and Banning and Indio, out into the desert. It is a bright late-winter day, and recent rains have greened the hills and coaxed the cacti into bloom. He keeps a sharp watch for landmarks: flatlands, dry lakes.

——I think this is the place. In fact, I'm sure of it.

He leaves the freeway and guides the car northeastward. Yes, no doubt of it: there's the ancient lakebed, and there's his abandoned automobile, looking ancient also, rusted and corroded, its hood up, its wheels and engine stripped by scavengers long ago.

He parks this car beside it, gets out, dons his backpack. He beckons to Claire.

——Let's go. We've got some hiking ahead of us.

She smiles timidly at him. She leaves the car and presses herself lightly against him, touching her lips to his. He begins to tremble.

——Claire. Oh, God, Claire.

——How far do we have to walk?

——Hours.

He gears his pace to hers. If necessary, they will camp overnight and go on into the city tomorrow, but he hopes they can get there before sundown. Claire is a strong hiker, and he is confident she can cover the distance in five or six hours, but there is always the possibility that he will fail to find the twin mesas. He has no compass points, no maps, nothing but his own intuitive sense of the city's location to guide him. They walk steadily northward. Neither of them says very much. Every half hour they pause to rest; he puts down his pack and she hands him the canteen. The air is mild and fragrant. Jackrabbits boldly accompany them. Blossoms are everywhere. Oxenshuer, transfigured by love, wants to leap and soar.

——We ought to be seeing those mesas soon.

——I hope so. I'm starting to get tired, John.

——We can stop and make camp if you like.

——No. No. Let's keep going. It can't be much farther, can it?

They keep going. Oxenshuer calculates they have covered twelve or thirteen kilometers already. Even allowing for some straying from course, they should be getting at least a glimpse of the mesas by this time, and it troubles him that they are not in view. If he fails to find them in the next half-hour, he will make camp, for he wants to avoid hiking after sundown.

Suddenly they breast a rise in the desert and the mesas come into view, two steep wedges of rock, dark gray against the sand. The shadows of late afternoon partially cloak them, but there is no mistaking them.

——There they are, Claire. Out there.

——Can you see the city?

——Not from this distance. We've come around from the side, somehow. But we'll be there before very long.

At a faster pace, now, they head down the gentle slope and into the flats. The mesas dominate the scene. Oxenshuer's heart pounds, not entirely from the strain of carrying his pack. Ahead wait Matt and Jean, Will and Nick, the Speaker, the god-house, the labyrinth. They will welcome Claire as his woman; they will give them a small house on the edge of the city; they will initiate her into their rites. Soon. Soon. The mesas draw near.

——Where's the city, John?

——Between the mesas.

——I don't see it.

——You can't really see it from the front. All that's visible is the palisade, and when you get very close you can see some rooftops above it.

——But I don't even see the palisade, John. There's just an open space between the mesas.

——A shadow effect. The eye is easily tricked.

But it does seem odd to him. At twilight, yes, many deceptions are possible; nevertheless he has the clear impression from here that there *is* nothing but open space between the mesas. Can these be the wrong mesas? Hardly. Their shape is distinctive and unique; he could never confuse those two jutting slabs with other formations. The city, then? Where has the city gone? With each step he takes he grows more perturbed. He tries to hide his uneasiness from Claire, but she is tense, edgy, almost panicky now, repeatedly asking him what has happened, whether they are lost. He reassures her as best he can. This is the right place, he tells her. Perhaps it's an optical illusion that the city is invisible, or perhaps some other kind of illusion, the work of the city folk.

——Does that mean they might not want us, John? And they're hiding their city from us?

——I don't know, Claire.

——I'm frightened.

——Don't be. We'll have all the answers in just a few minutes.

When they are about five hundred meters from the face of

the mesas, Claire's control breaks. She whimpers and darts forward, sprinting through the cacti toward the opening between the mesas. He calls out to her, tells her to wait for him, but she runs on, vanishing into the deepening shadows. Hampered by his unwieldy pack, he stumbles after her, gasping for breath. He sees her disappear between the mesas. Weak and dizzy, he follows her path, and in a short while comes to the mouth of the canyon.

There is no city.

He does not see Claire.

He calls her name. Only mocking echoes respond. In wonder he penetrates the canyon, looking up at the steep sides of the mesas, remembering streets, avenues, houses.

——Claire?

No one. Nothing. And now night is coming. He picks his way over the rocky, uneven ground until he reaches the far end of the canyon. He looks back at the mesas, and outward at the desert, and he sees no one. The city has swallowed her and the city is gone.

——Claire! Claire!

Silence.

He drops his pack wearily, sits for a long while, finally lays out his bedroll. He slips into it but does not sleep; he waits out the night, and when dawn comes he searches again for Claire, but there is no trace of her. All right. All right. He yields. He will ask no questions. He shoulders his pack and begins the long trek back to the highway.

By mid-morning he reaches his car. He looks back at the desert, ablaze with noon light. Then he gets in and drives away.

He enters his apartment on Hollywood Boulevard. From here, so many months ago, he first set out for the desert; now all has come round to the beginning again. A thick layer of dust covers the cheap utilitarian furniture. The air is musty. All the blinds are closed. He wanders aimlessly from hallway to living room, from living room to bedroom, from bedroom to kitchen, from kitchen to hallway. He kicks off his boots and sprawls out on the threadbare living-room carpet, face down, eyes closed. So tired. So drained. I'll rest a bit.

"John?"

It is the Speaker's voice.

"Let me alone," Oxenshuer says. "I've lost her. I've lost you. I think I've lost myself."

"You're wrong. Come to us, John."

"I did. You weren't there."

"Come now. Can't you feel the city calling you? The Feast is over. It's time to settle down among us."

"I couldn't find you."

"You were still lost in dreams then. Come now. Come. The saint calls you. Jesus calls you. Claire calls you."

"Claire?"

"Claire," he says.

Slowly Oxenshuer gets to his feet. He crosses the room and pulls the blinds open. This window faces Hollywood Boulevard; but, looking out, he sees only the red plains of Mars, eroded and cratered, glowing in purple noonlight. Vogel and Richardson are out there, waving to him. Smiling. Beckoning. The faceplates of their helmets glitter by the cold gleam of the stars. Come on, they call to him. We're waiting for you. Oxenshuer returns their greeting and walks to another window. He sees a lifeless wasteland here too. Mars again, or is it only the Mojave Desert? He is unable to tell. All is dry, all is desolate, all is beautiful with the serene transcendent beauty of desolation. He sees Claire in the middle distance. Her back is to him; she is moving at a steady, confident pace toward the twin mesas. Between the mesas lies the City of the Word of God, golden and radiant in the warm sunlight. Oxenshuer nods. This is the right moment. He will go to her. He will go to the city. The Feast of St. Dionysus is over, and the city calls to him.

Bring us together. Lead us to the ocean.
Help us to swim. Give us to drink.
Wine in my heart today,
Blood in my throat today,

Fire in my soul today,
All praise, O God, to thee.

Oxenshuer runs in long loping strides. He sees the mesas, he sees the city's palisade. The sound of far-off chanting throbs in his ears. "This way, brother!" Matt shouts. "Hurry, John!" Claire cries. He runs. He stumbles, and recovers, and runs again. Wine in my heart today. Fire in my soul today. "God is everywhere," the saint tells him. "But before all else, God is within you." The desert is a sea, the great warm cradling ocean, the undying mother-sea of all things, and Oxenshuer enters it gladly, and drifts, and floats, and lets it take hold of him and carry him wherever it will.

'KJWALLL'KJE'K'KOOTHAÏLLL'KJE'K

Roger Zelazny

After everyone had departed, the statements been taken, the remains of the remains removed—long after that, as the night hung late, clear, clean, with its bright multitudes doubled in their pulsing within the cool flow of the Gulf Stream about the station, I sat in a deck chair on the small patio behind my quarters, drinking a can of beer and watching the stars go by.

My feelings were an uncomfortable mixture, and I had not quite decided what to do with what was left.

It was awkward. I could make things neat and tidy again by deciding to forget the small inexplicables. I had accomplished what I had set out to do. I needed but stamp CLOSED on my mental file, go away, collect my fee, and live happily, relatively speaking, ever after.

No one would ever know or, for that matter, care about the little things that still bothered me. I was under no obligation to pursue matters beyond this point.

Except . . .

Maybe it *is* an obligation. At least, at times it becomes a compulsion, and one might as well salve one's notions of duty and free will by using the pleasanter term.

It? The possession of a primate forebrain, I mean, with a deep curiosity wrinkle furrowing it for better or worse.

I had to remain about the station awhile longer anyway, for appearances' sake.

I took another sip of beer.

Yes, I wanted more answers. To dump into the bottomless wrinkle up front there.

I might as well look around a bit more. Yes, I decided, I would.

I withdrew a cigarette and moved to light it. Then the flame caught my attention.

I stared at the flowing tongue of light, illuminating the palm and curved fingers of my left hand, raised to shield it from the night breeze. It seemed as pure as the starfires themselves, a molten, buttery thing, touched with orange, haloed blue, the intermittently exposed cherry-colored wick glowing, half-hidden, like a soul. And then the music began . . .

Music was the best term I had for it, because of some similarity of essence, although it was actually like nothing I had ever experienced before. For one thing, it was not truly sonic. It came into me as a memory comes, without benefit of external stimulus—but lacking that Lucite layer of self-consciousness that turns thought to recollection by touching it with time—as in a dream. Then, something suspended, something released, my feelings began to move to the effect. Not emotions, nothing that specific, but rather a growing sense of euphoria, delight, wonder, all poured together into a common body with the tide rising. What the progressions, what the combinations—what the thing was, truly—I did not know. It was an intense beauty, a beautiful intensity, however, and I was part of it. It was as if I were experiencing something no man had ever known before, something cosmic, magnificent, ubiquitous yet commonly ignored.

And it was with a peculiarly ambiguous effort, following a barely perceptible decision, that I twitched the fingers of my left hand sufficiently to bring them into the flame itself.

The pain broke the dream momentarily, and I snapped the lighter closed as I sprang to my feet, a gaggle of guesses passing through my head. I turned and ran across that humming artificial islet, heading for the small, dark cluster of buildings that held the museum, library, offices.

But even as I moved, something came to me again. Only this time it was not the glorious, musiclike sensation that had touched me moments earlier. Now it was sinister, bringing a fear that was none the less real for my knowing it to be irrational, to the accompaniment of sensory distortions that must have caused me to reel as I ran. The surface on which I moved buckled and swayed; the stars, the buildings, the ocean—everything—advanced and retreated in random, nauseating patterns of attack. I fell several times, recovered, rushed onward. Some of the distance I know that I crawled. Closing my eyes did no good, for everything was warped, throbbing, shifting, and awful inside as well as out.

It was only a few hundred yards, though, no matter what the signs and portents might say, and finally I rested my hands against the wall, worked my way to the door, opened it, and passed within.

Another door and I was into the library. For years, it seemed, I fumbled to switch on the light.

I staggered to the desk, fought with a drawer, wrestled a screwdriver out of it.

Then on my hands and knees, gritting my teeth, I crossed to the remote-access terminal of the Information Network. Slapping at the console's control board, I succeeded in tripping the switches that brought it to life.

Then, still on my knees, holding the screwdriver with both hands, I got the left side panel off the thing. It fell to the floor with a sound that drove spikes into my head. But the components were exposed. Three little changes and I could transmit, something that would eventually wind up in Central. I resolved that I would make those changes and send the two most damaging pieces of information I could guess at to the place where they might eventually be retrieved in association with something sufficiently similar to one day cause a query, a query that would hopefully lead to the destruction of that for which I was presently being tormented.

"I mean it!" I said aloud. "Stop right now! Or I'll do it!"

. . . And it was like taking off a pair of unfamiliar glasses: rampant reality.

I climbed to my feet, shut down the board.

The next thing, I decided, was to have that cigarette I had wanted in the first place.

With my third puff, I heard the outer door open and close.

Dr. Barthelme, short, tan, gray on top and wiry, entered the room, blue eyes wide, one hand partly raised.

"Jim! What's wrong?" he said.

"Nothing," I replied. "Nothing."

"I saw you running. I saw you fall."

"Yes. I decided to sprint over here. I slipped. Pulled a muscle. It's all right."

"Why the rush?"

"Nerves. I'm still edgy, upset. I had to run or something, to get it out of my system. Decided to run over and get a book. Something to read myself to sleep with."

"I can get you a tranquilizer."

"No, that's all right. Thanks. I'd rather not."

"What were you doing to the machine? We're not supposed to fool with—"

"The side panel fell off when I went past it. I was just going to put it back on." I waved the screwdriver. "The little setscrews must have jiggled loose."

"Oh."

I stooped and fitted it back into place. As I was tightening the screws, the telephone rang. Barthelme crossed to the desk, poked an extension button, and answered it.

After a moment, he said, "Yes, just a minute" and turned. "It's for you."

"Really?"

I rose, moved to the desk, took the receiver, dropping the screwdriver back into the drawer and closing it.

"Hello?" I said.

"All right," said the voice. "I think we had better talk. Will you come and see me now?"

"Where are you?"

"At home."

"All right. I'll come."

I hung up.

"Don't need that book after all," I said. "I'm going over to Andros for a while."

"It's pretty late. Are you certain you feel up to it?"

"Oh, I feel fine now," I said. "Sorry to have worried you."

He seemed to relax. At least, he sagged and smiled faintly.

"Maybe *I* should go take the trank," he said. "Everything that's happened . . . You know. You scared me."

"Well, what's happened has happened. It's all over, done."

"You're right, of course. . . . Well, have a good time, whatever."

He turned toward the door and I followed him out, extinguishing the light as I passed it.

"Good night, then."

"Good night."

He headed back toward his quarters, and I made my way down to the docking area, decided on the *Isabella*, got in. Moments later, I was crossing over, still wondering. Curiosity may ultimately prove nature's way of dealing with the population problem.

* * *

It was on May Day—not all that long ago, though it seems so—that I sat to the rear of the bar at Captain Tony's in Key West, to the right, near to the fireplace, drinking one of my seasonal beers. It was a little after eleven, and I had about decided that this one was a write-off, when Don came in through the big open front of the place. He glanced around, his eyes passing over me, located a vacant stool near the forward corner of the bar, took it, and ordered something. There were too many people between us, and the group had returned to the stage at the rear of the room behind me and begun another set, with a loud opening number. So, for a time, we just sat there—wondering, I guess.

After ten or fifteen minutes, he got to his feet and made his way back to the rest room, passing around the far side of the bar. A short while later, he returned, moving around my side. I felt his hand on my shoulder.

"Bill!" he said. "What are you doing down here?"

I turned, regarded him, grinned.

"Sam! Good Lord!"

We shook hands. Then, "Too noisy in here to talk," he said. "Let's go someplace else."

"Good idea."

I send one Christmas card each year. Instead of a signature, it bears a list of four bars and the cities in which they exist. Easter, May Day, the summer solstice and Halloween, I sit in those bars, from nine until midnight. I never miss two in a row. Neither does Don Walsh.

I always pay cash wherever I go because I do not exist, officially. There is no credit card, birth record, or passport for me. Some years back, when everything and everybody was being documented and recorded, I was part of the International Data Bank project. I suffered the Frigid Quicksand Effect—cold feet and a sinking feeling—at the last moment. So I tore up my punch cards, changed my face, and dropped out of existence.

It wasn't all that simple, of course. But I took advantage of my position; I employed my special skills. I worked things out most carefully.

There is a real world, which exists about us, within us, and there is its analogue, which exists in the data bank. The latter approximates the former with great consistency and an amazing profusion of accurate detail.

There are, of course, many points at which this image is somewhat less than perfect. Not everything is described, recorded, with total accuracy. There are tolerance rules, allowances for this situation, built into the system. I know because I helped put them there. There are also ways of getting information accepted into the system by means other than the normal input channels, ways that a knowledgeable person could even use to set up a temporary identity. I know this for the same reason.

And why? Why am I here, rather than here and there too? I guess I chose this way of life, sacrificing the real benefits of the programmed condition—and there are many—because I hated that other guy: the image, the parody of myself—economic, medical, social, mental, everything quantifiable—who would dance to the binary waltz like a windup doll with a painted-on smile until he stopped, at which time that too would be noted and united with the Great Statistic. And I hate him because I fear that I could easily become him, my smile also as predictable as a curve on a graph.

So now I have to make my living around the edges of things; and Don, who heads the second-largest detective agency in the world, is one of the means I employ.

After a time, we found ourselves on a dim and deserted stretch of beach, smelling the salty breath of the ocean, listening to it, and feeling an occasional droplet. We halted, and I lit a cigarette.

"Did you know that the Florida current carries over two million tons of uranium past here every year?" he said.

"To be honest, no," I told him.

"Well, it does. What do you know about dolphins?"

"That's better," I said. "They are beautiful, friendly creatures, so well adapted to their environment that they don't have to mess it up in order to lead the life they seem to enjoy. They are highly intelligent, they're cooperative, and they seem totally lacking in all areas of maliciousness. They—"

"That's enough." He raised his hand. "You like dolphins. I knew you would say that. You sometimes remind me of one—swimming through life, not leaving traces, retrieving things for me."

"Keep me in fish. That's all."

"A couple thousand for this one, varying upward in accordance with its complexity. But it should be a relatively easy, yes-or-no thing, and not take you too long. It's quite near here, as a matter of fact, and the incident is only a few days old."

"Oh? What's involved?"

"I'd like to clear a gang of dolphins of a homicide charge," he said.

If he expected me to say something, he was disappointed. I was thinking, recalling a news account from the previous week. Two scuba-clad swimmers had been killed in one of the undersea parks to the east, at about the same time that some very peculiar activity on the part of dolphins was being observed in the same area. The men had been bitten and chewed by something possessing a jaw configuration approximating that of *Tursiops truncatus,* the bottle-nosed dolphin, a normal visitor and sometime resident of these same parks. The particular park in which the incident occurred had been closed until further notice. There were no witnesses to the attack, as I recalled, and I had not come across any follow-up story.

"I'm serious," he finally said.

"One of those guys was a qualified guide who knew the area, wasn't he?"

He brightened, there in the dark.

"Yes," he said. "Michael Thornley. He used to do some moonlighting as a guide. He was a full-time employee of the Beltrane Processing people. Did underwater repair and maintenance of their extraction plants. Ex-Navy. Frogman. Extremely qualified. The other fellow was a landlubber friend of his from Andros. Rudy Myers. They went out together at an odd hour, stayed rather long. In the meantime, several dolphins were seen getting the hell out, fast. They leaped the 'wall,' instead of passing through the locks. Others used the normal exits. These were blinking on and off like mad. In a matter of a few minutes, actually, every dolphin in the park had apparently departed. When an employee went looking for Mike and Rudy, he found them dead."

"Where do you come into the picture?"

"The Institute of Delphinological Studies does not appreciate the bad press this gives to their subject. They maintain there has never been an authenticated case of an unprovoked attack by a dolphin on a human being. They are anxious not to have this go on record as one if it really isn't."

"Well, it hasn't actually been established. Perhaps something else did it. Scared the dolphins too."

"I have no idea," he said, lighting a cigarette of his own. "But it was not all that long ago that the killing of dolphins was finally made illegal throughout the world, and that the pioneer work of people like Lilly came to be appreciated, with a really large-scale project set up for the assessment of the creature. They have come up with some amazing results, as you must know. It is no longer a question of trying to demonstrate whether a dolphin is as intelligent as a man. It has been established that they are highly intelligent—although their minds work along radically different lines, so that there probably never can be a true comparison. This is the basic reason for the continuing communication problems, and it is also a matter of which the general public is pretty much aware. Given this, our client does not like the inferences that could be drawn from the incident—namely, that powerful, free-ranging creatures of this order of intelligence could become hostile to man."

"So the Institute hired you to look into it?"

"Not officially. I was approached because the character of the thing smacks of my sort of investigation specialties as well as the scientific. Mainly, though, it was because of the urgings of a wealthy little old lady who may someday leave the Institute a fortune: Mrs. Lydia Barnes, former president of the Friends of the Dolphin Society—the citizen group that had lobbied for the initial dolphin legislation years ago. She is really paying my fee."

"What sort of place in the picture did you have in mind for me?"

"Beltrane will want a replacement for Michael Thornley. Do you think you could get the job?"

"Maybe. Tell me more about Beltrane and the parks."

"Well," he said, "I guess it was a generation or so back that Dr. Spence at Harwell demonstrated that titanium hydroxide would create a chemical reaction that separated uranyl ions from seawater. It was costly, though, and it was not until years later that Samuel Beltrane came along with his screening technique, founded a small company, and quickly turned it into a large one, with uranium-extraction stations all along this piece of the Gulf Stream. While his process was quite clean, environmentally speaking, he was setting up in business at a time when public pressure on industry was such that some gesture of ecological concern was pretty much de rigueur. So he threw a lot of money, equipment and man-hours into the setting up of the four undersea parks in the vicinity of the island of Andros. A section of the barrier reef makes one of them especially attractive. He got a nice tax break on the deal. Deserved, though, I'd say. He cooperated with the Dolphin Studies people, and labs were set up for them in the parks. Each of the four areas is enclosed by a sonic 'wall,' a sound barrier that keeps everything outside out and everything inside in, in terms of the larger creatures. Except for men and dolphins. At a number of points, the 'wall' possesses 'sound locks'—a pair of sonic curtains, several meters apart—which are operated by means of a simple control located on the bottom. Dolphins are capable of teaching one another how to use it, and they are quite good about closing the door behind them. They come and go, visiting the labs at will, both learning from and, I guess, teaching the investigators."

"Stop," I said. "What about sharks?"

"They were removed from the parks first thing. The dolphins even helped chase them out. It has been over a decade now since the last one was put out."

"I see. What say does the company have in running the parks?"

"None, really. They service the equipment now, that's all."

"Do many of the Beltrane people work as park guides too?"

"A few, part-time. They are in the area, they know it well, they have all the necessary skills."

"I would like to see whatever medical reports there were."

"I have them here, complete with photos of the bodies."

"What about the man from Andros—Rudy Myers? What did he do?"

"He'd trained as a nurse. Worked in several homes for the aged. Taken in a couple times on charges of stealing from the patients. Charges dropped once. A suspended sentence the second time. Sort of blackballed from that line of work afterward. That was six or seven years back. Held a variety of small jobs then and kept a clean record. He had been working on the island for the past couple of years in a sort of bar."

"What do you mean 'sort of bar'?"

"It has only an alcohol license, but it serves drugs too. It's way out in the boonies, though, so nobody's ever raised a fuss."

"What's the place called?"

"The Chickcharny."

"What's that mean?"

"A piece of local folklore. A chickcharny is a sort of tree spirit. Mischievous. Like an elf."

"Colorful enough, I guess. Isn't Andros where Martha Millay, the photographer, makes her home?"

"Yes, it is."

"I'm a fan of hers. I like underwater photography, and hers is always good. In fact, she did several books on dolphins. Has anyone thought to ask her opinion of the killings?"

"She's been away."

"Oh. Hope she gets back soon. I'd like to meet her."

"Then you will take the job?"

"Yes, I need one just now."

He reached into his jacket, withdrew a heavy envelope, passed it to me.

"There you have copies of everything I have. Needless to say—"

"Needless to say," I said. "The life of a mayfly will be as eternity to them."

I slipped it into my own jacket and turned away.

"Be seeing you," I said.

"Leaving already?"

"I've a lot to do."

"Good luck, then."

"Thanks."

I went left and he went right, and that was that for then.

Station One was something of a nerve center for the area. That is, it was larger than the other extraction plants and contained the field office, several laboratories, a library, a museum, a dispensary, living quarters, and a few recreational features. It was an artificial island, a fixed platform about seven hundred feet across, and it monitored and serviced eight other plants within the area. It was within sight of Andros, largest of the Bahama Islands, and if you like plenty of water about you, which I do, you would find the prospect peaceful and more than a little attractive.

After the tour and introductions that first day, I learned that my duties were about one-third routine and two-thirds response to circumstances. The routine part was inspection and preventive maintenance. The rest was unforeseen repair, retrieval, and replacement work—general underwater handyman stuff whenever the necessity arose.

It was Dr. Leonard Barthelme, the Area Director, who met me and showed me around. A pleasant little fellow who seemed to enjoy talking about his work, middle-aged, a widower, he had made his home at Station One for almost five years. The first person to whom he introduced me was Frank Cashel, whom we found in the main laboratory, eating a sandwich and waiting for some test to run its course.

Frank swallowed and smiled, rose, and shook hands with me as Barthelme explained, "This is the new man, James Madison."

He was dark, with a touch of gray here and there, a few creases accentuating a ruggedness of jawline and cheekbone, the beginnings of a bulge above his belt.

"Glad to have you around," he said. "Keep an eye out for pretty rocks, and bring me a branch of coral every now and then. We'll get along fine."

"Frank's hobby is collecting minerals," Barthelme said. "The display in the museum is his. We'll pass that way in a few minutes and you can see it. Quite interesting."

I nodded.

"Okay. I'll remember. See what I can find you."

"Know anything about the subject?" Frank asked me.

"A little. I used to be something of a rock hound."

"Well, I'd appreciate it."

As we walked away, Barthelme remarked, "He makes some money on the side selling specimens at gem shows. I would bear that in mind before I gave him too much in the way of my spare time, or samples."

"Oh."

"What I mean is, if you feel like going in for that sort of thing on a more than occasional basis, you ought to make it clear that you want a percentage."

"I see. Thanks."

"Don't misunderstand me," he said. "He's a fine fellow. Just a little absentminded."

"How long has he been out here?"

"Around two years. Geophysicist. Very solid."

We stopped by the equipment shed then, where I met Andy Deems and Paul Carter: the former, thin and somewhat sinister in appearance because of a scribbling of scars on his left cheek, which a full beard did not completely conceal; the latter, tall, fair, smooth-faced, and somewhere between husky and fat. They were cleaning some tanks when we entered, and wiped their hands, shook mine, and said they were glad to meet me. They both did the same sort of work I would be doing, the normal staffing calling for four of us, working in pairs. The fourth man was Paul Vallons, who was currently out with Ronald Davies, the boatmaster, replacing an instrument package in a sampler buoy. Paul, I learned, had been Mike's partner, the two of them having been friends since their Navy days. I would be working with him much of the time.

"You will soon be reduced to this miserable state yourself," Carter said cheerfully, as we were leaving. "Enjoy your morning. Gather rosebuds."

"You are miserable because you sweat most obscenely," Deems observed.

"Tell it to my glands."

As we crossed the islet, Barthelme observed that Deems was the most capable underwater man he had ever met. He had lived in one of the bubble cities for a time, lost his wife and daughter in the *Rumoko II* disaster, and come topside to stay. Carter had come across from the West Coast about five months ago, immediately following a divorce or separation he did not care to talk about. He had been employed by Beltrane out there and had requested a transfer.

Barthelme took me through the second lab, which was vacant just then, so that I could admire the large, illuminated map of the seas about Andros, beads of light indicating the disposition and well-being of the devices that maintained the sonic 'walls' about the parks and stations. I saw that we were enclosed by a boundary that took in the nearest park also.

"In which one was the accident?" I asked.

He turned and studied my face, then pointed, indicating our own.

"It was farther in, over there," he said. "Toward the northeast end of the park. What have you heard about it?"

"Just the news report," I said. "Has anything new been discovered?"

"No. Nothing."

With my fingertip, I traced the reversed L of lights that outlined the area.

"No holes in the 'wall'?" I asked.

"There haven't been any equipment failures for a long while."

"Do you think it was a dolphin?"

He shrugged. Then, "I'm a chemist," he said, "not a dolphin specialist. But it strikes me, from everything I've read, that there are dolphins and there are dolphins. The average dolphin seems to be quite pacific, with an intelligence possibly equivalent to our own. Also, they should follow the same old normal distribution curve—the bulk of them in the middle, a few morons on one end, a few geniuses on the other. Perhaps a feebleminded dolphin who was not responsible for his actions did it. Or a Raskolnikov dolphin. Most of what is known about them comes from a study of average specimens. Statistically, in the relatively brief while such investigations have been going on, this has to be so. What do we know of their psychiatric abnormalities? Nothing, really." He shrugged again. "So yes, I think it is possible," he finished.

I was thinking then of a bubble city and some people I had never met, and I wondered whether dolphins ever felt rotten, guilty, and miserable as hell over anything they had done. I sent that thought back where it had come from, just as he said, "I hope you are not worried . . . ?"

"Curious," I said. "But concerned, too. Naturally."

He turned and, as I followed him to the door, said, "Well, you have to remember first that it was a good distance to the northeast, in the park proper. We have nothing operating over there, so your duties should not take you anywhere near the place where it occurred. Second, a team from the Institute of Delphinological Studies is searching the entire area, including our annex here, with underwater detection equipment. Third, until further notice there will be a continuing sonar scan about any area where one of our people has to submerge himself—and a shark cage and submersible decompression chamber will go along on all deep dives, just in case. The locks have all been closed until this is settled. And you will be given a weapon—a long metal tube carrying a charge and a shell—that should be capable of dispatching an angry dolphin or a shark."

I nodded.

"Okay," I said, as we headed toward the next cluster of buildings. "That makes me feel a lot better."

"I was going to get around to that in a little while anyway," he said. "I was looking for the best way to get into it, though. I feel better too. . . . This part is offices. Should be empty now."

He pulled open the door and I followed him through: desks, partitions, filing cabinets, office machines, water cooler—nothing unusual—and, as he had said, quite deserted. We passed along its center aisle and out the door at its far end, where we crossed the narrow breezeway that separated it from the adjacent building. We entered there.

"This is our museum," he said. "Sam Beltrane thought it

would be nice to have a small one to show visitors. Full of sea things as well as a few models of our equipment."

Nodding, I looked about. At least the model equipment did not dominate, as I would have expected. The floor was covered with green indoor-outdoor carpeting, and a miniature version of the station itself occupied a tablelike frame near the front door, all of its underside equipment exposed. Shelves on the wall behind it held larger-scale versions of some of the more important components, placarded with a paragraph or two of explanation and history. There were an antique cannon, two lantern frames, several belt buckles, a few coins, and some corroded utensils displayed nearby, salvaged from a centuries-old vessel that still lay on the bottom not very far from the station, according to the plaque. On the opposite wall, with several of the larger ones set up on frames before it, was a display of marine skeletons accompanied by colored sketches of the fully fleshed and finned versions, ranging from tiny spinefish to a dolphin, along with a full-sized mock-up of a shark, which I determined to come back and compare a little more carefully on my own time. There was a large section containing Frank Cashel's mineral display, neatly mounted and labeled, separated from the fish by a window and overlooked by a slightly awkward but still attractive watercolor titled *Miami Skyline,* with the name "Cashel" scrawled in its lower corner.

"Oh, Frank paints," I said. "Not bad."

"No, that's his wife, Linda's," he replied. "You will meet her in just a minute. She should be next door. She runs the library and takes care of all our clerical work."

So we passed through the door that led to the library and I saw Linda Cashel. She was seated at a desk, writing, and she looked up as we entered. She appeared to be in her mid-twenties. Her hair was long, sun-bleached, pulled back, held with a jeweled clip. Blue eyes, in a longish face with a cleft chin, a slightly upturned nose, a sprinkling of freckles, and some very even, very white teeth were displayed as Barthelme greeted her and introduced us.

". . . Anytime you want a book," she said.

I looked around at the shelves, the cases, the machines.

"We keep good copies of the standard reference works we use a lot," she said. "I can get facsimile copies of anything else on a day's notice. There are some shelves of general fiction and light stuff over there." She indicated a rack beside the front window. "Then there are those banks of cassettes to your right, mostly undersea noises—fish sounds and such, for part of a continuing study we do for the National Science Foundation—and the last bank is music, for our own enjoyment. Everything is catalogued here." She rose and slapped a file unit, indicated an index key taped to its side. "If you want to take something out and nobody's around, I would appreciate it if you would record its number, your name, and the date in this book." She glanced at a ledger on the corner of her desk. "And if you want to keep anything longer than a week, please mention it to me. There is also a tool chest in the bottom drawer, in case you ever need a pair of pliers. Remember to put them back. That covers everything I can think of," she said. "Any questions?"

"Doing much painting these days?" I asked.

"Oh," she said, reseating herself, "you saw my skyline. I'm afraid next door is the only museum I'll ever get into. I've pretty much quit. I know I'm not that good."

"I rather liked it."

She twisted her mouth.

"When I'm older and wiser and somewhere else, maybe I'll try again. I've done everything I care to with water and shorelines."

I smiled because I couldn't think of anything else to say, and she did the same. Then we left, and Barthelme gave me the rest of the morning off to get settled in my cottage, which had been Michael Thornley's quarters. I went and did that.

After lunch, I went to work with Deems and Carter in the equipment shed. As a result, we finished early. Since it was still too soon to think of dinner, they offered to take me for a swim, to see the sunken ship.

It was about a quarter mile to the south, outside the "wall," perhaps twenty fathoms down—what was left of it—and eerie, as such things always are, in the wavering beams we extended. A broken mast, a snapped bowsprit, a section of deck planking and smashed gunwale visible above the mud, an agitated horde of little fish we had disturbed at whatever they were about within and near the hulk, a partial curtain of weeds drawn and redrawn by the currents, and that was all that remained of someone's hopes for a successful voyage, some shipbuilders' labors, and possibly a number of people whose last impressions were of storm or sword, and then the gray, blue, green, sudden springs uncoiling, cold.

Or maybe they made it over to Andros and dinner, as we did later. We ate in a red-and-white-checked-tablecloth sort of place near to the shore, where just about everything man-made clung, the interior of Andros being packed with mangrove swamps, mahogany and pine forests, doves, ducks, quail, pigeons, and chickcharnies. The food was good; I was hungry.

We sat for a time afterward, smoking and talking. I still had not met Paul Vallons, but I was scheduled to work with him the following day. I asked Deems what he was like.

"Big fellow," he said, "around your size, only he's good-looking. Kind of reserved. Fine diver. He and Mike used to take off every weekend, go helling around the Caribbean. Had a girl on every island, I'll bet."

"How's he—taking things?"

"Pretty well, I guess. Like I said, he's kind of reserved, doesn't show his feelings much. He and Mike had been friends for years."

"What do you think got Mike?"

Carter broke in then.

"One of those damned dolphins," he said. "We should never have started fooling with them. One of them came up under me once, damn near ruptured me."

"They're playful," Deems said. "It didn't mean any harm."

"I think it did. And that slick skin of theirs reminds me of a wet balloon. Sickening!"

"You're prejudiced. They're friendly as puppies. It probably goes back to some sexual hangup."

"Crap!" Carter said. "They—"

Since I had gotten it started, I felt obligated to change the subject. So I asked whether it was true that Martha Millay lived nearby.

"Yes," Deems said, taking hold of the opportunity. "She has a place about four miles down the coast from here. Very neat, I understand, though I've only seen it from the water. Her own little port. She has a hydrofoil, a sailboat, a good-sized cabin cruiser, and a couple little power launches. Lives alone in a long, low building right smack on the water. Not even a road out that way."

"I've admired her work for a long while. I'd like to meet her sometime."

He shook his head.

"I'll bet you never do. She doesn't like people. Doesn't have a listed phone."

"That's a pity. Any idea why she's that way?"

"Well . . ."

"She's deformed," Carter said. "I met her once, on the water. She was at anchor and I was going past on my way to one of the stations. That was before I knew about her, so I went near, just to say hello. She was taking pictures through the glass bottom of her boat, and when she saw me she started to scream and holler for me to get away, that I was scaring the fish. And she snatched up a tarp and pulled it over her legs. I got a look, though. She's a nice, normal-looking woman from the waist up, but her hips and legs are all twisted and ugly. I was sorry I'd embarrassed her. I was just as embarrassed myself, and I didn't know what to say. So I yelled, 'Sorry' and waved and kept going."

"I heard she can't walk at all," Deems said, "though she is supposed to be an excellent swimmer. I've never seen her myself."

"Was she in some sort of accident, do you know?"

"Not as I understand it," he said. "She is half-Japanese, and the story I heard is that her mother was a Hiroshima baby. Some sort of genetic damage."

"Pity."

"Yes."

We settled up and headed back. Later, I lay awake for a long while, thinking of dolphins, sunken ships, drowned people, half-people, and the Gulf Stream, which kept talking to me through the window. Finally, I listened to it, and it took hold of me and we drifted away together into the darkness to wherever it finally goes.

Paul Vallons was, as Andy Deems had said, around my size and good-looking, in a dark, clothing-advertisement sort of way. Another twenty years and he would probably even look distinguished. Some guys win all the way around. Deems had also been right about his reserve. He was not especially talkative, although he managed this without seeming unfriendly. As for his diving prowess, I was unable to confirm it that first day I worked with him, for we pulled shore duty while Deems and Carter got sent over to Station Three. Back to the equipment shed . . .

I did not think it a good idea to ask him about his late buddy, or dolphins, which pretty much confined me conversation-wise to the business at hand and a few generalities. Thus was the morning passed.

After lunch, though, as I began thinking ahead, going over my plans for that evening, I decided he would be as good as anyone when it came to getting directions to the Chickcharny.

He lowered the valve he had been cleaning and stared at me.

"What do you want to go to that dive for?" he asked.

"Heard the place mentioned," I said. "Like to see it."

"They serve drugs without a license," he told me. "No inspection. If you like the stuff, you have no guarantee you won't be served some crap the village idiot cooks up in an outhouse."

"Then I'll stick to beer. Still like to see the place."

He shrugged.

"Not that much to look at. But here—"

He wiped his hands, tore an old leaf from the back of the wall calendar, and sketched me a quick map. I saw that it was a bit inland, toward the birds and mangroves, muck and mahogany. It was also somewhat to the south of the place I had been the previous evening. It was located on a stream, built up on pilings out over the water, he said, and I could take a boat right up to the pier that adjoined it.

"Think I'll go over tonight," I said.

"Remember what I said."

I nodded as I tucked away the map.

The afternoon passed quickly. There came a massing of clouds, a brief rainfall—about a quarter-hour's worth—and then the sun returned to dry the decks and warm the just-rinsed world. Again, the workday ended early for me, by virtue of our having run out of business. I showered quickly, put on fresh clothes, and went to see about getting the use of a light boat.

Ronald Davies, a tall, thin-haired man with a New England accent, said I could take the speedboat called *Isabella,* complained about his arthritis, and told me to have a good time. I nodded, turned her toward Andros, and sputtered away, hoping the Chickcharny included food among its inducements, as I did not want to waste time by stopping elsewhere.

The sea was calm and the gulls dipped and pivoted, uttering hoarse cries, as I spread the wings of my wake across their preserve. I really had no idea what it was that I was going after. I did not like operating that way, but there was no alternative. I had no real line of attack. There was no handle on this one. I had determined, therefore, to simply amass as much information as I could as quickly as possible. Speed always seems particularly essential when I have no idea what it is that might be growing cold.

Andros enlarged before me. I took my bearings from the place we had eaten the previous evening, then sought the mouth of the stream Vallons had sketched for me.

It took me about ten minutes to locate it, and I throttled down and made my way slowly up its twisting course. Occasionally, I caught a glimpse of a rough roadway running along the bank to my left. The foliage grew denser, however, and I finally lost sight of it completely. Eventually, the boughs met overhead, locking me for several minutes into an alley of premature twilight, before the stream widened again, took me around a corner, and showed me the place as it had been described.

I headed to the pier, where several other boats were moored, tied up, climbed out, and looked around. The building to my right—the only building, outside of a small shed—did extend out over the water, was a wood-frame job, and was so patched that I doubted any of its original materials remained. There were half a dozen vehicles parked beside it, and a faded sign named the place THE CHICKCHARNY. Looking to my left as I advanced, I could see that the road which had accompanied me was in better shape than I would have guessed.

Entering, I discovered a beautiful mahogany bar about fifteen feet ahead of me, looking as if it might have come from some ship. There were eight or ten tables here and there, several of them occupied, and a curtained doorway lay to the right of the bar. Someone had painted a crude halo of clouds above it.

I moved up to the bar, becoming its only occupant. The bartender, a fat man who had needed a shave yesterday as well as the day before, put down his newspaper and came over.

"What'll it be?"

"Give me a beer," I said. "And can I get something to eat?"

"Wait a minute."

He moved farther down, checked a small refrigerator.

"Fish-salad sandwich?" he said.

"Okay."

"Good. Because that's all we've got."

He put it together, brought it over, drew me my beer.

"That was your boat I heard, wasn't it?" he asked.

"That's right."

"Vacationing?"

"No. I just started work over at Station One."

"Oh. Diver?"

"Yes."

He sighed.

"You're Mike Thornley's replacement, then. Poor guy."

I prefer the word "successor" to "replacement" in these situations, because it makes people seem less like sparkplugs. But I nodded.

"Yeah, I heard all about it," I said. "Too bad."

"He used to come here a lot."

"I heard that, too—and that the guy he was with worked here."

He nodded.

"Rudy. Rudy Myers," he said. "Worked here a couple years."

"They were pretty good friends, huh?"

He shook his head.

"Not especially," he said. "They just knew each other. Rudy worked in back." He glanced at the curtain. "You know."

I nodded.

"Chief guide, high medical officer, and head bottle washer," he said, with rehearsed levity. "You interested . . . ?"

"What's the specialty of the house?"

"Pink Paradise," he said. "It's nice."

"What's it got?"

"Bit of a drift, bit of an up, the pretty lights."

"Maybe next time," I said. "Did he and Rudy go swimming together often?"

"No, that was the only time. You worried?"

"I am not exactly happy about it. When I took this job nobody told me I might get eaten. Did Mike ever say anything about unusual marine activity or anything like that?"

"No, not that I can recall."

"What about Rudy? Did he like the water?"

He peered at me, working at the beginnings of a frown.

"Why do you ask?"

"Because it occurs to me that it might make a difference. If he was interested in things like that and Mike came across something unusual, he might take him out to see it."

"Like what?"

"Beats the hell out of me. But if he found something and it was dangerous, I'd like to know about it."

The frown went away.

"No," he said. "Rudy wouldn't have been interested. He wouldn't have walked outside to look if the Loch Ness monster was swimming by."

"Wonder why he went, then?"

He shrugged.

"I have no idea."

I had a hunch that if I asked him anything else I just might ruin our beautiful rapport. So I ate up, drank up, paid up, and left.

I followed the stream out to the open water again and ran south along the coast. Deems had said it was about four miles that way, figuring from the restaurant, and that it was a long, low building right on the water. All right. I hoped she had returned from that trip Don had mentioned. The worst she could do was tell me to go away. But she knew an awful lot that might be worth hearing. She knew the area and she knew dolphins. I wanted her opinion, if she had one.

There was still a lot of daylight left in the sky, though the air seemed to have cooled a bit, when I spotted a small cove at about the proper distance, throttled down, and swung toward it. Yes, there was the place, partway back and to the left, built against a steep rise and sporting a front deck that projected out over the water. Several boats, one of them a sailboat, rode at rest at its side, sheltered by the long, white curve of a breakwater.

I headed in, continuing to slow, and made my way around the inward point of the breakwall. I saw her sitting on the pier, and she saw me and reached for something. Then she was lost to sight above me as I pulled into the lee of the structure. I killed my engine and tied up to the handiest piling, wondering each moment whether she would appear the next, boathook in hand, ready to repel invaders.

This did not happen, though, so I climbed out and onto a ramplike staging that led me topside. She was just finishing adjusting a long, flaring skirt, which must have been what she had been reaching after. She wore a bikini top, and she was seated on the deck itself, near to the edge, legs tucked out of sight beneath the green, white and blue print material. Her hair was long and very black, her eyes dark and large. Her features were regular, with a definite Oriental cast to them, of the sort I find exceedingly attractive. I paused at the top of the ramp, feeling immediately uncomfortable as I met her gaze.

"My name is Madison, James Madison," I said. "I work out at Station One. I'm new there. May I come up for a minute?"

"You already have," she said. Then she smiled, a tentative thing. "But you can come the rest of the way over and have your minute."

So I did, and as I advanced she kept staring at me. It made me acutely self-conscious, a condition I thought I had mastered shortly after puberty, and as I was about to look away, she said, "Martha Millay—just to make it a full introduction," and she smiled again.

"I've admired your work for a long while," I said, "although that is only part of the reason I came by. I hoped you could help me to feel safer in my own work."

"The killings," she said.

"Yes. Exactly. Your opinion. I'd like it."

"All right. You can have it," she said. "But I was on Martinique at the time the killings occurred, and my intelligence comes only from the news reports and one phone conversation with a friend at the IDS. On the basis of years of acquaintanceship, years spent photographing them, playing with them, knowing them—loving them—I do not believe it possible that a dolphin would kill a human being. The notion runs contrary to all my experience. For some peculiar reason—perhaps some delphinic concept as to the brotherhood of self-conscious intelligence—we seem to be quite important to them, so important that I even believe one of them might rather die himself than see one of us killed."

"So you would rule out even a self-defense killing by a dolphin?"

"I think so," she said, "although I have no facts to point at here. However, what is more important, in terms of your real question, is that they struck me as very undolphinlike killings."

"How so?"

"I don't see a dolphin as using his teeth in the way that was described. The way a dolphin is designed, his rostrum—or beak—contains a hundred teeth, and there are eighty-eight in his lower jaw. But if he gets into a fight with, say, a shark or a whale, he does not use them for purposes of biting or slashing. He locks them together, which provides a very rigid structure, and uses his lower jaw, which is considerably undershot, for purposes of ramming his opponent. The anterior of the skull is quite thick and the skull itself sufficiently large to absorb enormous shocks from blows administered in this fashion—and they are tremendous blows, for dolphins have very powerful neck muscles. They are quite capable of killing sharks by battering them to death. So even granting for the sake of argument that a dolphin might have done such a thing, he would not have bitten his victims. He would have bludgeoned them."

"So why didn't someone from the Dolphin Institute come out and say that?"

She sighed.

"They did. The news media didn't even use the statement they gave them. Apparently nobody thought it an important enough story to warrant any sort of follow-up."

She finally took her eyes off me and stared out over the water.

Then, "I believe their indifference to the damage caused by running only the one story is more contemptible even than actual malice," she finally said.

Acquitted for a moment by her gaze, I lowered myself to sit on the edge of the pier, my feet hanging down over the side. It had been an added discomfort to stand, staring down at her. I joined her in looking out across her harbor.

"Cigarette?" I said.

"I don't smoke."

"Mind if I do?"

"Go ahead."

I lit one, drew on it, thought a moment, then asked, "Any idea as to how the deaths might have occurred?"

"It could have been a shark."

"But there hasn't been a shark in the area for years. The 'walls'—"

She laughed.

"There are any number of ways a shark could have gotten in," she said. "A shift on the bottom, opening a tunnel or crevice beneath the 'wall.' A temporary short circuit in one of the projectors that didn't get noticed—or a continuing one, with a short somewhere in the monitoring system. For that matter, the frequencies used in the 'wall' are supposed to be extremely distressing to many varieties of marine life, but not necessarily fatal. While a shark would normally seek to avoid the 'wall,' one could have been driven, forced through by some disturbance, and then found itself trapped inside."

"That's a thought," I said. "Yes . . . Thank you. You didn't disappoint me."

"I would have thought that I had."

"Why?"

"All that I have done is try to vindicate the dolphins and show that there is possibly a shark inside. You said that you wanted me to tell you something that would make you feel safer in your work."

I felt uncomfortable again. I had the sudden, irrational feeling that she somehow knew all about me and was playing games at that moment.

"You said that you are familiar with my work," she said suddenly. "Does that include the two picture books on dolphins?"

"Yes. I enjoyed your text, too."

"There wasn't that much of it," she said, "and it has been several years now. Perhaps it was too whimsical. It has been a long while since I've looked at the things I said. . . ."

"I thought them admirably suited to the subject—little Zen-like aphorisms for each photograph."

"Can you recall any?"

"Yes," I said, one suddenly coming to me, "I remember the shot of the leaping dolphin, where you caught his shadow over the water and had for a caption, 'In the absence of reflection, what gods . . .' "

She chuckled briefly.

"For a long while I thought that that one was perhaps too cute. Later, though, as I got to know my subject better, I decided that it was not."

"I have often wondered as to what sort of religion or religious feelings they might possess," I said. "It has been a common element among all the tribes of man. It would seem that something along these lines appears whenever a certain level of intelligence is achieved, for purposes of dealing with those things that are still beyond its grasp. I am baffled as to the forms it might take among dolphins, but quite intrigued by the notion. You say you have some ideas on it?"

"I have done a lot of thinking as I watched them," she said, "attempting to analyze their character in terms of their behavior, their physiology. Are you familiar with the writings of Johan Huizinga?"

"Faintly," I said. "It has been years since I read *Homo Ludens*, and it struck me as a rough draft for something he never got to work out completely. But I recall his basic premise as being that culture begins as a sort of sublimation of a play instinct, elements of sacred performances and festal contests continuing for a time in the evolving institutions, perhaps always remaining present at some level—although his analysis stopped short of modern times."

"Yes," she said. "The play instinct. Watching them sport about, it has often seemed to me that as well adapted as they are to their environment, there was never a need for dolphins to evolve complex social institutions, so that whatever it was they did possess along those lines was much closer to the earlier situations considered by Huizinga—a life condition filled with an overt indulgence in their version of festal performances and contests."

"A play-religion?"

"Not quite that simple, though I think that is part of the picture. The problem here lies in language. Huizinga employed the Latin word *ludus* for a reason. Unlike the Greek language, which had a variety of words for idling, for competing in contests, for passing the time in different fashions, Latin reflected the basic unity of all these things and summarized them into a single concept by means of the word *ludus*. The dolphins' distinctions between play and seriousness are obviously different from our own, just as ours are different from the Greeks'. In our understanding of the meaning of *ludus*, however, in our ability to realize that we may unify instances of activity from across a broad spectrum of behavior patterns by considering them as a form of play, we have a better basis for conjecture as well as interpretation."

"And in this manner you have deduced their religion?"

"I haven't, of course. I only have a few conjectures. You say you have none?"

"Well, if I had to guess, just to pull something out of the air, I would say some form of pantheism—perhaps something akin to the less contemplative forms of Buddhism."

"Why 'less contemplative'?" she asked.

"All that activity," I said. "They don't even really sleep, do they? They have to get topside quite regularly in order to breathe. So they are always moving about. When would they be able to drift beneath the coral equivalent of a bo tree for any period of time?"

"What do you think your mind would be like if you never slept?"

"I find that rather difficult to conceive. But I imagine I would find it quite distressing after a while, unless . . ."

"Unless what?"

"Unless I indulged in periodic daydreaming, I suppose."

"I think that might be the case with dolphins, although with a brain capacity such as they possess I do not feel it need necessarily be a periodic thing."

"I don't quite follow you."

"I think they are sufficiently endowed to do it simultaneously with other thinking, rather than serially."

"You mean always dreaming a little? Taking their mental vacations, their reveries, sidewise in time as it were?"

"Yes. We do it too, to a limited extent. There is always a little background thinking, a little mental noise going on while we are dealing with whatever thoughts are most pressing in our consciousness. We learn to suppress it, calling this concentration. It is, in one sense, a process of keeping ourselves from dreaming."

"And you see the dolphin as dreaming and carrying on his normal mental business at the same time?"

"In a way, yes. But I also see the dreaming itself as a somewhat different process."

"In what way?"

"Our dreams are largely visual in nature, for our waking lives are primarily visually oriented. The dolphin, on the other hand—"

"—is acoustically oriented. Yes. Granting this constant dreaming effect and predicating it on the neurophysiological structures they possess, it would seem that they might splash around enjoying their own sound tracks."

"More or less, yes. And might not this behavior come under the heading of *ludus*?"

"I just don't know."

"One form of *ludus*, which the Greeks of course saw as a separate activity, giving it the name *diagōge*, is best translated as mental recreation. Music was placed in this category, and Aristotle speculated in his *Politics* as to the profit to be derived from it, finally conceding that music might conduce to virtue by making the body fit, promoting a certain ethos, and enabling us to enjoy things in the proper way—whatever that means. But considering an acoustical daydream in this light—as a musical variety of *ludus*—I wonder if it might not indeed promote a certain ethos and foster a particular way of enjoying things?"

"Possibly, if they were shared experiences."

"We still have no proper idea as to the meanings of many of their sounds. Supposing they are vocalizing some part of this experience?"

"Perhaps, given your other premises."

"Then that is all I have," she said. "I choose to see a religious significance in spontaneous expressions of *diagōge*. You may not."

"I don't. I'd buy it as a physiological or psychological necessity, even see it—as you suggested—as a form of play, or *ludus*. But I have no way of knowing whether such musical activity is truly a religious expression, so for me the ball stops rolling right there. At this point, we do not really understand their ethos or their particular ways of viewing life. A concept as alien and sophisticated as the one you have outlined would be well-nigh impossible for them to communicate to us, even if the language barrier were a lot thinner than it is now. Short of actually finding a way of getting inside them to know it for oneself, I do not see how we can deduce religious sentiments here, even if every one of your other conjectures is correct."

"You are, of course, right," she said. "The conclusion is not scientific if it cannot be demonstrated. I cannot demonstrate it, for it is only a feeling, an inference, an intuition—and I offer it only in that spirit. But watch them at their play sometime, listen to the sounds your ears will accept. Think about it. Try to feel it."

I continued to stare at the water and the sky. I had already learned everything I had come to find out and the rest was just frosting, but I did not have the pleasure of such desserts every day. I realized then that I liked the girl even more than I had thought I would, that I had grown quite fascinated as she had spoken, and not entirely because of the subject. So, partly to prolong things and partly because I was genuinely curious, I said, "Go ahead. Tell me the rest. Please."

"The rest?"

"You see a religion or something on that order. Tell me what you think it must be like."

She hesitated. Then, "I don't know," she said. "The more one compounds conjectures the sillier one becomes. Let us leave it at that."

But that would leave me with little to say but "Thank you" and "Good night." So I pushed my mind around inside the parameters she had laid down, and one of the things that came to me was Barthelme's mention of the normal distribution curve with reference to dolphins.

"If, as you suggest," I began, "they constantly express and interpret themselves and their universe by a kind of subliminal dreamsong, it would seem to follow that, as in all things, some are better at it than others. How many Mozarts can there be, even in a race of musicians? Champions, in a nation of athletes? If they all play at a religious *diagōge*, it must follow that some are superior players. Would they be priests or prophets? Bards? Holy singers? Would the areas in which they dwell be shrines, holy places? A dolphin Vatican or Mecca? A Lourdes?"

She laughed.

"Now *you* are getting carried away, Mr.—Madison."

I looked at her, trying to see something beyond the apparently amused expression with which she faced me.

"You told me to think about it," I said; "to try to feel it."

"It would be strange if you were correct, would it not?"

I nodded.

"And probably well worth the pilgrimage," I said, standing, "if only I could find an interpreter. I thank you for the minute I took and the others you gave me. Would you mind terribly if I dropped by again sometime?"

"I am afraid I am going to be quite busy," she said.

"I see. Well, I appreciate what you have given me. Good night, then."

"Good night."

I made my way back down the ramp to the speedboat, brought it to life, guided it about the breakwall and headed toward the darkening sea, looking back only once, in hopes of discovering just what it was that she called to mind, sitting there, looking out across the waves. Perhaps the Little Mermaid, I decided.

She did not wave back to me. But then it was twilight, and she might not have noticed.

Returning to Station One, I felt sufficiently inspired to head for the office/museum/library cluster to see what I could pick up in the way of reading materials having to do with dolphins.

I made my way across the islet and into the front door, passing the shadow-decked models and displays of the museum and turning right. I swung the door open. The light was on in the library, but the place was empty. I found several books that I had not read listed, so I hunted them up, leafed through them, settled on two, and went to sign them out.

As I was doing this, my eyes were drawn toward the top of the ledger page by one of the names entered there: Mike Thornley. I glanced across at the date and saw that it happened to be the day before his death. I finished signing out my own materials and decided to see what it was he had taken to read on the eve of his passing. Well, read and listen to. There were three items shown, and the prefix to one of the numbers indicated that it had been a tape.

The two books turned out to be light popular novels. When I checked the tape, however, a very strange feeling possessed me. It was not music, but rather one from the marine-biology section. Verily. To be precise, it was a recording of the sounds of the killer whale.

Even my pedestrian knowledge of the subject was sufficient, but to be doubly certain, I checked in one of the books I had right there with me. Yes, the killer whale was undoubtedly the dolphin's greatest enemy, and well over a generation ago experiments had been conducted at the Naval Undersea Center in San Diego, using the recorded sounds of the killer whale to frighten dolphins, for purposes of developing a device to scare them out of tuna nets, where they were often inadvertently slaughtered.

What could Thornley possibly have wanted it for? Its use in a waterproof broadcasting unit could well have accounted for the unusual behavior of the dolphins in the park at the time he was killed. But why? Why do a thing like that?

I did what I always do when I am puzzled: I sat down and lit a cigarette.

While this made it even more obvious to me that things were not what they had seemed at the time of the killings, it also caused me once again to consider the apparent nature of the attack. I thought of the photos I had seen of the bodies, of the medical reports I had read.

Bitten. Chewed. Slashed.

Arterial bleeding, right carotid . . .

Severed jugular; numerous lacerations of shoulders and chest . . .

According to Martha Millay, a dolphin would not go about it that way. Still, as I recalled, their many teeth, while not enormous, were needle-sharp. I began paging through the books, looking for photographs of the jaws and teeth.

Then the thought came to me, with dark, more than informational overtones to it: *There is a dolphin skeleton in the next room.*

Mashing out my cigarette, I rose then, passed through the doorway into the museum, and began looking about for the light switch. It was not readily apparent. As I sought it, I heard the door on the other side of the room open.

Turning, I saw Linda Cashel stepping across the threshold. With her next step, she looked in my direction, froze, and muffled the beginning of a shriek.

"It's me. Madison," I said. "Sorry I alarmed you. I'm looking for the light switch."

Several seconds passed. Then, "Oh," she said. "It's down in back of the display. I'll show you."

She crossed to the front door, groped behind a component model.

The lights came on, and she gave a nervous laugh.

"You startled me," she said. "I was working late. An unusual thing, but I got backed up. I stepped out for a breath of air and didn't see you come in."

"I've got the books I was looking for," I said, "but thanks for finding me the switch."

"I'll be glad to sign them out for you."

"I already did that," I said, "but I left them inside because I wanted to take another look at the display before I went home."

"Oh. Well, I was just going to close up. If you want to stay awhile, I'll let you do it."

"What does it consist of?"

"Just turning out the lights and closing the doors—we don't lock them around here. I've already shut the windows."

"Sure, I'll do that. I'm sorry I frightened you."

"That's all right. No harm done."

She moved to the front door, turned when she reached it, and smiled again, a better job this time.

"Well, good night."

"Good night."

My first thought was that there were no signs of any extra

work having come in since the last time I had been around, my second one was that she had been trying a little too hard to get me to believe her, and my third thought was ignoble.

But the proof of the pudding would keep. I turned my attention to the dolphin skeleton.

The lower jaw, with its neat, sharp teeth, fascinated me, and its size came close to being its most interesting feature. Almost, but not quite. The most interesting thing about it had to be the fact that the wires which held it in place were clean, untarnished, bright and gleaming at their ends, as if they had just recently been cut—unlike their more oxidized brethren everyplace else where the specimen had been wired.

The thing I found interesting about the size was that it was just about right to make it a dandy hand weapon.

And that was all. That was enough. But I fingered the maxillary and premaxillary bones, running my hand back toward the blowhole; I traced the rostrum; I gripped the jaw once more. Why, I did not really know for a moment, until a grotesque vision of Hamlet filtered into my mind. Or was it really that incongruous? A phrase out of Loren Eiseley came to me then: ". . . We are all potential fossils still carrying within our bodies the crudities of former existences, the marks of a world in which living creatures flow with little more consistency than clouds from age to age." We came from the water. This fellow I gripped had spent his life there. But both our skulls were built of calcium, a sea product chosen in our earlier days and irrevocably part of us now; both were housings for large brains—similar, yet different; both seemed to contain a center of consciousness, awareness, sensitivity, with all the concomitant pleasures, woes, and available varieties of conclusions concerning existence which that entailed, passing at some time or other within these small, rigid pieces of carbonate of lime. The only really significant difference, I suddenly felt, was not that this fellow had been born a dolphin and I a man, but only, rather, that I still lived—a very minor point in terms of the time-scale onto which I had wandered. I withdrew my hand, wondering uncomfortably whether my remains would ever be used as a murder weapon.

Having no further reason for being there, I collected my books, closed up, and cleared out.

Returning to my cottage, I deposited the books on my bed table and left the small light burning there. I departed again by means of the back door, which let upon a small, relatively private patio, pleasantly situated right at the edge of the islet with an unobstructed view of the sea. But I did not pause to admire the prospect just then. If other people might step out for a breath of air, so could I.

I strolled until I located a suitable spot, a small bench in the shadow of the dispensary. I seated myself there, fairly well hidden, yet commanding a full view of the complex I had but recently quitted. For a long while I waited, feeling ignoble, but watching anyway.

As the minutes continued their parade, I came near to deciding that I had been mistaken, that the margin of caution had elapsed, that nothing would occur.

But then the door at the far end of the office—the one through which I had entered on my initial tour of the place—opened, and the figure of a man emerged. He headed toward the nearest shore of the islet, then commenced what would have seemed but the continuance of a stroll along its edge to anyone just noticing him then. He was tall, around my height, which narrowed the field considerably, so that it was really almost unnecessary for me to wait and see him enter the cottage that was assigned to Paul Vallons, and after a moment see the light go on within.

A little while later, I was in bed with my dolphin books, reflecting that some guys seem to have it made all the way around; and puzzling and wondering, with the pied typecase Don had handed me, that I was ever born to set it right.

The following morning, during the ambulatory, coffee-tropism phase of preconsciousness, I stumbled across the most damnable, frightening item in the entire case. Or rather, I stepped over it—perhaps even on it—before its existence registered itself. There followed an appreciable time-lag, and then its possible significance occurred to me.

I stooped and picked it up: an oblong of stiff paper, an envelope, which had apparently been pushed in beneath the back door. At least, it lay near to it.

I took it with me to the kitchenette table, tore it open, extracted and unfolded the paper it contained. Sipping my coffee, I read over the block-printed message several times:

AFFIXED TO THE MAINMAST OF THE WRECK, ABOUT A FOOT BENEATH THE MUD.

That was all. That was it.

But I was suddenly fully awake. It was not just the message, as intriguing as I naturally found it, but the fact that someone had selected me as its recipient. Who? And why?

Whatever it was—and I was certain there was something—I was most disturbed by the implication that someone was aware of my extraordinary reasons for being there, with the necessary corollary that that person knew too much about me. My hackles rose, and the adrenaline tingles came into my extremities. No man knew my name; a knowledge of it jeopardized my existence. In the past, I had even killed to protect my identity.

My first impulse was to flee, to throw over the case, dispose of this identity and lose myself in the manner in which I had become adept. But then I would never know, would never know when, where, how, why, and in what fashion I had been tripped up, found out. And most important, by whom.

Also, considering the message again, I had no assurance that flight would be the end of things for me. For was there not an element of coercion here? Of tacit blackmail in the implied imperative? It was as if the sender were saying, *I know. I will assist. I will keep silent. For there is a thing you will do for me.*

Of course I would go and inspect the wreck, though I would have to wait until the day's work was done. No use speculating as to what I would find, although I would handle it most gingerly. That gave me the entire day in which to consider what I might have done wrong, and to decide upon the best means of defending myself. I rubbed my ring, where the death-spores slept, then rose and went to shave.

Paul and I were sent over to Station Five that day. Standard inspection and maintenance work. Dull, safe, routine. We scarcely got wet.

He gave no indication of knowing that I was on to anything. In fact, he even started several conversations. In one, he asked me, "Did you get over to the Chickcharny?"

"Yes," I said.

"What did you think of it?"

"You were right. A dive."

He smiled and nodded. Then, "Try any of their specialties?" he asked.

"Just had a few beers."

"That was safest," he said. "Mike—my friend who died—used to go there a lot."

"Oh?"

"I used to go with him at first. He'd take something and I'd sit around and drink and wait for him to come down."

"You didn't go in for it yourself?"

He shook his head.

"Had a bad experience when I was younger. Scared me. Anyway, so did he—there, I mean—several times, at the Chickcharny. He used to go in back—it's a sort of ashram back there. Did you see it?"

"No."

"Well, he had a couple bad ones in there and we got in an argument about it. He knew the damn place wasn't licensed, but he didn't care. I finally told him he ought to keep a safe supply at the station, but he was worried about the damn company regulations against it. Which I think was silly. Anyhow, I finally told him he could go by himself if he wanted to go that badly and couldn't wait till the weekend to go someplace else. I stopped going."

"Did he?"

"Only recently," he said. "The hard way."

"Oh."

"So if you do go in for it, I'm telling you the same thing I told him: Keep your own around if you can't wait to go someplace farther and cleaner than that."

"I'll remember," I said, wondering then whether he might, perhaps, be on to something about me and be encouraging my breaking the company rules for purposes of getting rid of me. That seemed kind of far out, though, a little too paranoiac a reaction on my part. So I dismissed it.

"Did he have any more bad ones?" I asked.

"I think so," he said. "I don't really know."

And that was all he had to say on the subject. I wanted to ask him more things, of course, but our acquaintanceship was still such that I knew I would need an opening to get through, and he didn't give me any.

So we finished up, returned to Station One, went our separate ways. I stopped by and told Davies I wanted a boat later. He assigned me one, and I returned to my cottage and waited until I saw him leave for dinner. Then I went back to the docks, threw my diving gear into the boat, and took off. This elaboration was necessary because of the fact that solo diving was against the rules, and also because of the safety precautions Barthelme had enunciated to me that first day. True, they applied only inside the area and the ship lay outside it, but I did not care to explain where I was going either.

The thought had of course occurred to me that it might be a trap, set to spring in any of a number of ways. While I hoped my friend in the museum still had his lower jaw in place, I did not discount the possibility of an underwater ambush. In fact, I had one of the little death rods along with me, all loaded and primed. The photos had been quite clear. I did not forget. Nor did I discount the possibility of a booby trap. I would simply have to be very careful in my poking about.

While I did not know what would happen if I were spotted solo-diving with company gear, I would have to count on my ability to talk or lie my way out of it, if catching me in this breach of domestic tranquillity was what the note's author had had in mind.

I came to what I thought to be the spot, anchored there, slipped into my gear, went over the side and down.

The cool smoothness held me and I did my dance of descent, curious, wary, with a heightened feeling of fragility. Toward the bottom then, with steady, sweeping movements down, I passed from cool to cold and light to dark. I switched on my torch, shot the beam about.

Minutes later, I found it, circled it, hunting about the vicinity for signs of fellow intruders.

But no, nothing. I seemed to be alone.

I made my way toward the hulk then, casting my light down the splintered length of the short-snapped mainmast. Small fish appeared, staging an unruly demonstration in the neighborhood of the gunwale. My light fell upon the layer of ooze at the base of the mast. It appeared undisturbed, but then I have no idea as to how long it takes ooze to settle.

Coming up beside/above it then, I probed it with a thin rod I had brought along. After several moments, I was satisfied that there was a small, oblong object, probably metallic, about eight inches beneath the surface.

Drawing nearer, I scooped away a layer. The water muddied, fresh material moving to fill the site of my excavation. Cursing mentally, I extended my left hand, fingers at full flex, slowly, carefully, down into the mud.

I encountered no obstacles until I reached the box itself. No wires, strings, foreign objects. It was definitely metal, and I traced its outline: about six by ten by three inches. It was up-ended and held in place against the mast by a double strand of wire. I felt no connections with anything else, so I uncovered it—at least momentarily—for a better look.

It was a small, standard-looking strongbox, handles on both ends and on the top. The wires ran through two of these loops. I shook out a coil of plastic cord and knotted it through the nearest one. After paying out a considerable length of it, I leaned down and used the pliers I had carried with me to sever the wires that held the box to the mast. Upward then, playing out the rest of the line behind me.

Back in the boat and out of my gear, I hauled it, hand over hand, up from the depths. The movement, the pressure changes did not serve to set anything off, so I felt a little safer in handling it when I finally brought it aboard. I set it on the deck and thought about it as I unfastened and recoiled the line.

The box was locked, and whatever was inside shifted around when I moved it. I sprung the lock with a screwdriver. Then I went over the side into the water, and holding on, reaching from there, I used the rod to flip back the lid.

But for the lapping of the waves and the sounds of my breathing, there was silence. So I reboarded and took a look inside.

It contained a canvas bag with a fold-down flap that snapped closed. I unsnapped it.

Stones. It was filled with dozens of rather undistinguished-looking stones. But since people generally have a reason for going to that much trouble, there had to be a decent intrinsic value involved. I dried off several of them, rubbing them vigorously with my towel. Then I turned them around every which way. Yes, there were a few glints, here and there.

I had not been lying to Cashel when he had asked me what I knew about minerals and I had said, "A little." Only a little. But in this instance it seemed that it might be enough. Selecting the most promising specimen for the experiment, I chipped away at the dirty minerals that sheathed the stone. Several minutes later, an edge of the material I had exposed exhibited great scratching abilities with the various materials on which I tested it.

So someone was smuggling diamonds and someone else wanted me to know about it. What did my informant expect me to do with this information? Obviously, if he had simply wanted the authorities informed he would have done it himself.

Knowing that I was being used for purposes I did not yet understand, I decided to do what was probably expected of me, inasmuch as it coincided with what I would have done anyhow.

I was able to dock and unload the gear without encountering any problems. I kept the bag of stones wrapped in my towel until I was back in my cottage. No more messages had been slipped beneath the door, so I repaired to the shower stall and cleaned myself up.

I couldn't think of anyplace really clever to hide the stones, so I stuffed the bag down into the garbage-disposal unit and replaced the drain cover. That would have to do. Before stashing it, though, I removed four of the ugly ducklings. Then I dressed and took a walk.

Strolling near, though, I saw that Frank and Linda were eating out on their patio, so I returned to my place and made myself a quick, prefabricated meal. Afterward, I watched the sun in its descending for perhaps twenty minutes. Then, what seemed an adequate period having passed, I made my way back again.

It was even better than I had hoped for. Frank sat alone, reading, on the now-cleared patio. I moved up and said, "Hello."

He turned toward me, smiled, nodded, lowered his book.

"Hello, Jim," he said. "Now that you've been here a few days, how do you like it?"

"Oh, fine," I said. "Just fine. How is everything with you?"

He shrugged.

"Can't complain. We were going to ask you over to dinner. Perhaps tomorrow?"

"Sounds great. Thanks."

"Come by about six?"

"All right."

"Have you found any interesting diversions yet?"

"Yes. As a matter of fact, I took your advice and resurrected my old rock-hounding habits."

"Oh? Come across any interesting specimens?"

"It just happens that I did," I said. "It was really an amazing accident. I doubt whether anybody would have located them except by accident. Here. I'll show you."

I dug them out of my pocket and dumped them into his hand.

He stared. He fingered them. He shifted them around. For perhaps half a minute.

Then, "You want to know what they are, is that it?" he asked.

"No. I already know that."

"I see."

He looked at me and smiled.

"Where did you find them?"

I smiled, very slowly.

"Are there more?" he asked.

I nodded.

He moistened his lips. He returned the stones.

"Well, tell me this if you will—what sort of deposit was it?"

Then I thought faster than I had at any time since my arrival. It was something about the way he had asked it that put my mind to spinning. I had been thinking purely in terms of a diamond-smuggling operation, with him as the natural disposer of the contraband stones. Now, though, I reviewed what scanty knowledge I did possess on the subject. The largest mines in the world were those of South Africa, where diamonds were found embedded in that rock known as kimberlite, or "blue ground." But how did they get there in the first place? Through volcanic action—as bits of carbon that had been trapped in streams of molten lava, subjected to intense heat and pressure that altered their structure to the hard, crystalline form of a girl's best friend. But there were also alluvial deposits—diamonds that had been cut free from their resting places by the actions of ancient streams, often borne great distances from their points of origin, and accumulated in offshore pockets. That was Africa, of course, and while I did not know much offhand as to New World deposits, much of the Caribbean island system had been built up by means of volcanic activity. The possibility of local deposits—of the volcanic-pipe variety or alluvial—was not precluded.

In view of my somewhat restricted area for activity since my arrival, I said, "Alluvial. It wasn't a pipe, I'll tell you that."

He nodded.

"Have you any idea as to the extent of your find?" he inquired.

"Not really," I said. "There are more where these came from. But as to the full extent of their distribution, it is simply too early for me to tell."

"Most interesting," he said. "You know, it jibes with a notion I've long held concerning this part of the world. You wouldn't care to give me just a very rough, general sort of idea as to what part of the ocean these are from, would you?"

"Sorry," I said. "You understand."

"Of course, of course. Still, how far would you go from here for an afternoon's adventure?"

"I suppose that would depend on my own notions on this

matter—as well as available air transportation, or hydrofoil."

He smiled.

"All right. I won't press you any further. But I'm curious. Now that you've got them, what are you going to do with them?"

I took my time lighting a cigarette.

"Get as much as I can for them and keep my mouth shut, of course," I finally said.

He nodded.

"Where are you going to sell them? Stop passers-by on the street?"

"I don't know," I said. "I haven't thought that much about it yet. I suppose I could take them to some jeweler's."

He chuckled.

"If you're very lucky. If you're lucky, you'll find one willing to take a chance. If you're very lucky, you'll find one willing to take a chance and also willing to give you a fair deal. I assume you would like to avoid the creation of a record, the crediting of extra income to your master account? Taxable income?"

"As I said, I would like to get as much as I can for them."

"Naturally. Then am I correct in assuming that your purpose in coming to me over this might somehow be connected with this desire?"

"In a word, yes."

"I see."

"Well?"

"I am thinking. To act as your agent for something like this would not be without risks of its own."

"How much?"

"No, I'm sorry," he said then. "It is probably too risky altogether. After all, it is illegal. I'm a married man. I could jeopardize my job by getting involved in something like this. If it had come along perhaps fifteen years ago . . . well, who knows? I'm sorry. Your secret is safe. Don't worry about that. But I would just as soon not be party to the enterprise."

"You are certain of that?"

"Positive. The return would have to be quite high for me even to consider it."

"Twenty percent?" I said.

"Out of the question."

"Maybe twenty-five . . ." I said.

"No. Twice that would scarcely—"

"Fifty percent? You're crazy!"

"Please! Keep your voice down! You want the whole station to hear?"

"Sorry. But that's out of the question. Fifty percent! No. If I can find a willing jeweler, I'll still be better off—even if he does cheat me. Twenty-five percent is tops. Absolutely."

"I am afraid I can't see it."

"Well, I wish you would think about it anyway."

He chuckled.

"It will be difficult to forget," he said.

"Okay. Well, I'll be seeing you."

"Tomorrow, at six."

"Right. Good night."

"Good night."

So I began walking back, reflecting on the possible permutations of people and events leading up to and culminating in the killings. But there were still too many gaps in the picture for me to come up with anything I really liked.

I was most troubled, of course, by the fact that there was someone who was aware that my presence actually represented more than its outward appearance. I searched my mind again and again for possible giveaways, but I did not see where I could have slipped up. I had been quite careful about my credentials. I had encountered no one with whom I had ever been familiar. I began wishing, not for the first time—nor, I was certain, the last—that I had not accepted this case.

I considered then what I ought to be about next, to push the investigation further along. I supposed I could inspect the place where the bodies had been found. I had not been there yet, mainly because I doubted there would be anything to be learned from it. Still . . . I put that on my list for the morrow, if I could hit it before dinner with the Cashels. If not, then the next day.

I wondered whether I had done the expected thing as to the

stones. I felt that I had, and I was very curious as to the repercussions—almost, but not quite, as curious as I was concerning the motives of my informant. Nothing I could do at the moment, though, but wait.

Thinking these thoughts, I heard myself hailed by Andy Deems from where he stood near his cottage, smoking his pipe. He wondered whether I was interested in a game of chess. I wasn't, really, but I went over anyhow. I lost two and managed to stalemate him on the third one. I felt very uncomfortable around him, but at least I didn't have to say much.

The following day, Deems and Carter were sent over to Station Six, while Paul and I took our turn at "miscellaneous duties as assigned" in and about the equipment shed. Another time-marking episode, I had decided, till I got to my real work once more.

And so it went, until late afternoon, when I was beginning to wonder what sort of cook Linda Cashel might be. Barthelme hurried into the shed.

"Get your gear together," he said. "We have to go out."

"What's the matter?" Paul asked him.

"Something is wrong with one of the sonic generators."

"What?"

He shook his head.

"No way of telling till we've brought it back and checked it over. All I know is that a light's gone out on the board. I want to pull the whole package and put in a new unit. No attempt at underwater repair work on this one, even if it looks simple. I want to go over it very carefully in the lab."

"Where is it situated?"

"To the southwest, at about twenty-eight fathoms. Go look at the board if you want. It will give you a better picture. But don't take too long, all right? There are a lot of things to load."

"Right. Which vessel?"

"The *Mary Ann*."

"The new deepwater rules . . . ?"

"Yes. Load everything. I'm going down to tell Davies now. Then I'm going to change clothes. I'll be back shortly."

"See you then."

"Yes."

He moved away and we set to work, getting our own gear, the shark cage, and the submersible decompression chamber ready to go. We made two trips to the *Mary Ann* then, took a break to go see the map, learned nothing new from it, and returned for the DC, which was stored on a cart.

"Ever been down in that area before?" I asked Paul as we began maneuvering the cart along.

"Yes," he said. "Some time back. It is fairly near to the edge of a submarine canyon. That's why there's a big bite out of that corner of the 'wall.' It plunges pretty sharply right beyond that section of the perimeter."

"Will that complicate things any?"

"It shouldn't," he said, "unless a whole section broke loose and carried everything down with it. Then we would have to anchor and hook up a whole new housing, instead of just switching the guts. That would take us somewhat longer. I'll review the work with you on the unit we'll be taking out."

"Good."

Barthelme rejoined us about then. He and Davies, who would also be going along, helped get everything stowed. Twenty minutes later, we were on our way.

The winch was rigged to lower both the shark cage and the decompression chamber tandem-fashion and in that order. Paul and I rode the DC down, keeping the extra lines from tangling, playing our lights about as we descended. While I had never had to use one, I had always found the presence of a decompression chamber on the bottom a thing of comfort, despite its slightly ominous function for the sort of work we would be doing. It was good to know that if I were injured I could get inside, signal, and be hauled directly to the top with no delays for decompression stops, the bottomside pressure being maintained in the bell's chamber on the way up and gradually returned to normal as they rushed me back to the dispensary. A heartening thought for all that, timewise.

Bottomside, we positioned the cage near to the unit, which

we found still standing, exhibiting no visible signs of damage, and we halted the illuminated DC a couple of fathoms up and off to the east. We were indeed on the edge of a steep cliff. While Paul inspected the sonic-broadcast unit, I moved nearer and flashed my light downward.

Jutting rocky pinnacles and twisting crevices . . . Reflexively, I drew back from the edge of the abyss, turned my light away. I returned and watched Paul work.

It took him ten minutes to disconnect the thing and free it from its mountings. Another five saw it secured and rising on its lines.

A bit later, in the periodic sweep of our beams, we caught sight of the replacement unit on the way down. We swam up to meet it and guided it into place. This time, Paul let me go to work. I indicated by pantomime that I wanted to, and he wrote on his slate: GO AHEAD SEE WHAT YOU REMEMB.

So I fastened it in place, and this took me about twenty minutes. He inspected the work, patted me on the shoulder, and nodded. I moved to connect the systems then, but stopped to glance at him. He indicated that I should go ahead.

This only took a few minutes, and when I was finished I had a certain feeling of satisfaction thinking of that light going on again on the big board back at the station. I turned around to indicate that the job was done and that he could come admire my work.

But he was no longer with me.

For a few seconds I froze, startled. Then I began shining my light around.

No, no. Nothing . . .

Growing somewhat panicky, I moved to the edge of the abyss and swept downward with the light. Luckily, he was not moving very quickly. But he was headed downward, all right. I took off after him as fast as I could move.

Nitrogen narcosis, deepwater sickness, or "rapture of the deep" does not usually hit at depths above 200 feet. Still, we were at around 170, so it was possible, and he certainly seemed to be showing the symptoms.

Worrying then about my own state of mind, I reached him,

caught him by the shoulder, turned him back. Through his mask, I could see the blissful expression that he wore.

Taking him by the arm and shoulder, I began drawing him back with me. For several seconds he accompanied me, offering no resistance.

Then he began to struggle. I had anticipated this possibility and shifted my grips into a *kwansetsu-waza* position, but quickly discovered that judo is not exactly the same underwater, especially when a tank valve is too near your mask or mouthpiece. I had to keep twisting my head away, pulling it back. For a time, it became impossible to guide him that way. But I refused to relinquish my grip. If I could just hold him a while longer and did not get hit by narcosis myself, I felt that I had the advantage. After all, his coordination was affected as well as his thinking.

I finally got him to the DC—a wild antenna of bubbles rising from his air hose by then, as he had spat out his mouthpiece and there was no way I could get it back in without letting go. Still, it might have been one of the reasons he became easier to manage near the end there. I don't know.

I stuffed him into the lighted chamber, followed, and got the hatch sealed. He gave up about then and began to sag. I was able to get his mouthpiece back into place, and then I threw the pull-up switch.

We began to rise almost immediately, and I wondered what Barthelme and Davies were thinking at that moment.

They got us up very quickly. I felt a slight jarring as we came to rest on the deck. Shortly afterward, the water was pumped out. I don't know what the pressure was up to—or down to—at that point, but the communicator came alive and I heard Barthelme's voice as I was getting out of my gear.

"We'll be moving in a few minutes," he said. "What happened, and how serious is it?"

"Nitrogen narcosis, I'd say. Paul just started swimming out and down, struggled with me when I tried to bring him back."

"Was either of you hurt?"

"No, I don't think so. He lost his mouthpiece for a little while, but I got it back in and he's breathing."

"What shape is he in otherwise?"

"Still rapturing, I'd guess. Sort of collapsed, drunken look to him."

"All right. You might as well get out of your gear—"

"I already have."

"—and get him out of his."

"Just starting."

"We'll radio ahead and have a medic hop out and be waiting at the dispensary, just in case. Sounds like what he really needs most is the chamber, though. So we'll just take it slow and easy in getting him back to surface pressure. I'm making an adjustment right now. . . . Do you have any rapture symptoms yourself?"

"No."

"Okay, there. We'll leave it at this setting for a little while now. . . . Is there anything else I should know?"

"Not that I can think of."

"All right, then. I'm going forward to radio for the doctor. If you want me for anything, whistle into the speaker. That should carry."

"Right."

I got Paul out of his rig then, hoping he would start coming around soon. But he didn't.

He just sat there, slouched, mumbling, eyes open but glassy. Every now and then he smiled.

I wondered what was wrong. If the pressure was indeed diminished, the recovery should have been almost instantaneous. Probably needed one more step, I decided.

But—

Could he have been down much earlier that morning, before the workday began?

Decompression time does depend upon the total amount of time spent underwater during about a twelve-hour period, since you are dealing with the total amount of nitrogen absorbed by the tissues, particularly the brain and spinal cord. Might he have been down looking for something, say, in the mud, at the base of a broken mast, amid the wreckage of a certain old vessel? Perhaps down for a long while, searching carefully, worried? Knowing that he had shore duty today, that there should be no more nitrogen accumulated during this workday? Then, suddenly, an emergency, and he has to chance it. He takes it as easy as possible, even encouraging the new man to go ahead and finish up the job. Resting, trying to hang on . . .

It could well be. In which case, Barthelme's decompression values were off. The time is measured from surface to surface, and the depth is reckoned from the deepest point reached in any of the dives. Hell, for all I knew he might have visited several caches spotted at various points along the ocean's bottom.

I leaned over, studied the pupils of his eyes—catching his attention, it seemed, in the process.

"How long were you down this morning?" I asked.

He smiled.

"Wasn't," he said.

"It doesn't matter what was involved. It's your health we're worried about now. How long were you down? What depths?"

He shook his head.

"Wasn't," he said.

"Damn it! I know you were! It was the old wreck, wasn't it? That's maybe twenty fathoms. So how long? An hour? Were you down more than once?"

"Wasn't down!" he insisted. "Really, Mike! I wasn't."

I sighed, leaned back. Maybe, possibly, he was telling the truth. People are all different inside. Perhaps his physiology was playing some other variation of the game than the one I had guessed at. It had been so neat, though. For a moment, I had seen him as the supplier of the stones and Frank as the fence. Then I had gone to Frank with my find, Frank had mentioned this development to him, and Paul, worried, had gone off while the station slept to make certain that things were still where they were supposed to be. His tissues accumulated a lot of nitrogen during his frantic searching, and then this happened. It certainly struck me as logical. But if it were me, I would have admitted to having been down. I could always come up with some lie as to the reason later.

"Don't you remember?" I tried again.

He commenced an uninspired stream of curses, but lost his enthusiasm before a dozen or so syllables. His voice trailed off. Then, "Why don't you b'lieve me, Mike? I wasn't down . . ."

"All right, I believe you," I said. "It's okay. Just take it easy."

He reached out and took hold of my arm.

"It's all beautiful," he said.

"Yeah."

"Everything is just—like it's never been before."

"What did you take?" I asked him.

". . . Beautiful."

"What are you on?" I insisted.

"You know I never take any," he finally said.

"Then what's causing it, whatever it is? Do you know?"

"Damn fine . . ." he said.

"Something went wrong on the bottom. What was it?"

"I don't know! Go away! Don't bring it back. . . . This is how it should be. Always. . . . Not that crap you take . . . Started all the trouble . . ."

"I'm sorry," I said.

". . . That started it."

"I know. I'm sorry. Spoiled things," I ventured. "Shouldn't have."

". . . Talked," he said. ". . . Blew it."

"I know. I'm sorry. But we got him," I tried.

"Yeah," he said. Then, "Oh, my God!"

"The diamonds. The diamonds are safe," I suggested quickly.

"Got him . . . Oh, my God! I'm sorry!"

"Forget it. Tell me what you see," I said, to get his mind back where I wanted it.

"The diamonds . . ." he said.

He launched into a long, disjointed monologue. I listened. Every now and then I said something to return him to the theme of the diamonds, and I kept throwing out Rudy Myers' name. His responses remained fragmentary, but the picture did begin to emerge.

I hurried then, trying to learn as much as I could before Barthelme returned and decompressed us any further. I was afraid that it would sober him up suddenly, because decompression works that way when you hit the right point in nitrogen-narcosis cases. He and Mike seemed to have been bringing in the diamonds, all right—from where, I did not learn. Whenever I tried to find out whether Frank had been disposing of them for them, he began muttering endearments to Linda. The part I hammered away most at began to come clear, though.

Mike must have said something one time, in the ashram back of the Chickcharny. It must have interested Rudy sufficiently so that he put together a specialty of the house other than a Pink Paradise for him—apparently, several times. These could have been the bad trips I had heard about. Whatever Rudy served him, he got the story out of him and saw dollar signs. Only Paul proved a lot tougher than he had thought. When he made his request for hush money and Mike told Paul about it, Paul came up with the idea for the mad dolphin in the park and got Mike to go along with it, persuading Rudy to meet him there for a payoff. Then things got sort of hazy, because the mention of dolphins kept setting him off. But he had apparently waited at a prearranged point, and the two of them took care of Rudy when that point was reached, one holding him, the other working him over with the jawbone. It was not clear whether Mike was injured fighting with Rudy and Paul then decided to finish him off and make him look like a dolphin slashee also, or whether he had planned that part carefully too and simply turned on Mike afterward, taking him by surprise. Either way, their friendship had been declining steadily for some time and the blackmail business had driven the final nail into the lid.

That was the story I got, punctuated rather than phrased by his responses to my oblique questioning. Apparently, killing Mike had bothered him more than he had thought it would, also. He kept calling me Mike, kept saying he was sorry, and I kept redirecting his attention.

Before I could get any more out of him, Barthelme came back and asked me how he was doing.

"Babbling," I replied. "That's all."

"I'm going to decompress some more. That might straighten

him out. We're on our way now, and there will be someone waiting."

"Good."

But it did not straighten him out. He remained exactly the same. I tried to take advantage, to get more out of him—specifically, the source of the diamonds—but something went wrong. His nirvana switched over to some version of hell.

He launched himself at my throat, and I had to fight him off, push him back, hold him in place. He sagged then, commenced weeping, and began muttering of the horrors he was witnessing. I talked slowly, softly, soothingly, trying to guide him back to the earlier, happier part of things. Nothing worked until I shut up, though. So I stayed silent and kept my guard up.

He drowsed then, and Barthelme continued to decompress us. I kept an eye on Paul's breathing and checked his pulse periodically, but nothing seemed amiss in that area.

We were fully decompressed by the time we docked, and I undogged the hatch and chucked out our gear. Paul stirred at that, opened his eyes, stared at me, then said, "That was weird."

"How do you feel now?"

"All right, I think. But very tired and kind of shaky."

"Let me give you a hand."

"Thanks."

I helped him out and assisted him down the plank to a waiting wheelchair. A young doctor was there, as were the Cashels, Deems, and Carter. I could not help wondering what was going on at the moment inside Paul's head. The doctor checked his heartbeat, pulse, blood pressure, shined a light into his eyes and ears, and had him touch the tip of his nose a couple of times. Then he nodded and gestured, and Barthelme began wheeling him toward the dispensary. The doctor walked along part of the way, talking with them. Then he returned while they went on, and he asked me to tell him everything that had happened.

So I did, omitting only the substance I had derived from the babbling part. Then he thanked me and turned toward the dispensary once more.

I caught up with him quickly, though.

"What does it look like?" I asked.

"Nitrogen narcosis," he replied.

"Didn't it take a rather peculiar form?" I said. "I mean, the way he responded to decompression and all?"

He shrugged.

"People come in all shapes and sizes, inside as well as out," he said. "Do a complete physical on a man and you still can't tell what he'd be like if he got drunk, say—loud, sad, belligerent, sleepy. The same with this. He seems to be out of it now, though."

"No complications?"

"Well, I'm going to do an EKG as soon as we get him to the dispensary. But I think he's all right. Listen, is there a decompression chamber in the dispensary?"

"Most likely. But I'm new here. I'm not certain."

"Well, why don't you come along until we find out? If there isn't one, I'd like to have that submersible unit moved over."

"Oh?"

"Just a precaution. I want him to stay in the dispensary overnight, with someone around to keep an eye on him. If there should be a recurrence, I want the machine handy so he can be recompressed right away."

"I see."

We caught up with Barthelme at the door. The others were there also.

"Yes, there is a unit inside," Barthelme told him, "and I'll sit up with him."

Everyone volunteered, though, and the night was finally divided into three shifts—Barthelme, Frank, and Andy, respectively. Each of them, of course, was quite familiar with decompression equipment.

Frank came up and touched my arm.

"Nothing much we can really do here now," he said. "Shall we go have that dinner?"

"Oh?" I said, automatically glancing at my watch.

"So we eat at seven instead of six-thirty," he said, chuckling.

"Fine. That will give me time to shower and change."

"Okay. Come right over as soon as you're ready. We'll still have time for a drink."

"All right. I'm thirsty. See you soon."

I went on back to my place and got cleaned up. No new billets-doux, and the stones were still in the disposal unit. I combed my hair and started back across the islet.

As I neared the dispensary, the doctor emerged, talking back over his shoulder to someone in the doorway. Barthelme, probably. As I approached, I saw that he was carrying his bag.

He withdrew, began to move away. He nodded and smiled when he saw me.

"I think your friend will be all right," he said.

"Good. That is just what I was going to ask you."

"How do you feel?"

"All right. Fine, actually."

"You have had no symptoms at all. Correct?"

"That's right."

"Fine. If you were to, you know where to go. Right?"

"Indeed."

"Okay, then. I'll be going now."

"So long."

He headed off toward a tiny hopper he had landed near the main lab. I continued on over to Frank's place.

Frank came out to meet me.

"What did the doctor have to say?" he asked.

"That everything looks all right," I told him.

"Uh-huh. Come on in and tell me what you're drinking."

He opened the door, held it.

"A bourbon would be nice," I said.

"With anything?"

"Just ice."

"Okay. Linda's out back, setting things on the table."

He moved about, putting together a pair of drinks. I wondered whether he was going to say anything about the diamond business now, while we were alone. But he didn't.

He turned, passed me my drink, raised his in a brief salute, took a sip.

"Tell me all about it," he said then.

"All right."

The telling lasted into dinner and out of it again. I was very hungry, Linda was quite quiet, and Frank kept asking questions, drawing out every detail of Paul's discomfort, distress. I wondered about Linda and Frank. I could not see her keeping her affair secret on a small place like the station. What did Frank really know, think, feel about it? What was the true function of their triangle in this bizarre case?

I sat with them for a while after dinner, and I could almost feel the tension between the two of them, a thing he seemed set on dealing with by keeping the conversation moving steadily along the lines he had established, she by withdrawing from it. I had no doubt that it had been precipitated by Paul's mishap, but I came to feel more and more awkward in my role as a buffer against an approaching quarrel, a confrontation, or the renewal of an old one. Thanking them for the meal, I excused myself as soon as I could, pleading a weariness that was half-real.

Frank got to his feet immediately.

"I'll walk you back," he said.

"All right."

So he did.

As we neared my place, he finally said it.

"About those stones . . ."

"Yes?"

"You're sure there are lots more where they came from?"

"Come this way," I said, leading him around the cottage to the patio and turning when we reached it. "Just in time for the last couple of minutes of sunset. Beautiful. Why don't you watch it finish up? I'll be right back."

I let myself in through the rear door, moved to the sink, and got the disposal unit open. It took me a minute or so to work the bag out. I opened it, seized a double fistful, and carried them back outside.

"Cup your hands," I said to him.

He did, and I filled them.

"How's that?"

He raised them, moved nearer the light spilling through the open door.

"My God!" he said. "You really do!"

"Of course."

"All right. I'll dispose of them for you. Thirty-five percent."

"Twenty-five is tops. Like I said."

"I know of a gem-and-mineral show a week from Saturday. A man I know could be there if I gave him a call. He'd pay a good price. I'll call him—for thirty percent."

"Twenty-five."

"It's a pity we are so close and can't quite come to terms. We both lose that way."

"Oh, all right. Thirty it is."

I took back the stones and dumped them into my pockets, and we shook on it. Then Frank turned.

"I'm going over to the lab now," he said. "See what's the matter with that unit you brought back."

"Let me know when you find out, will you? I'd like to know."

"Sure."

So he went away and I restashed the gems, fetched a dolphin book, and began to page through it. Then it struck me just how funny it was, the way things were working out. All the talk about dolphins, all my reading, speculating, including a long philosophical dissertation on their hypothetical dreamsongs as a religio-diagogical form of *ludus*—for what? To find that it was probably all unnecessary? To realize that I would probably get through the entire case without even seeing a dolphin?

Well, that was what I had wanted, of course, what Don and Lydia Barnes and the Institute wanted—for me to clear the good name of the dolphin. Still, what a tangled mess it was turning out to be! Blackmail, murder, diamond smuggling, with a little adultery tossed in on the side . . . How was I going to untangle it sweetly and neatly, clear the suspects—who were out practicing their *ludus* and not giving a damn about the whole business—and then fade from the picture, as is my wont, without raising embarrassing questions, without seeming to have been especially involved?

A feeling of profound jealousy of the dolphin came over me and did not entirely vanish. Did they ever create problem situations of this order among themselves? I strongly doubted it. Maybe if I collected enough green karma stamps I could put in for dolphin next time around. . . .

Everything caught up with me, and I dozed off with the light still burning.

A sharp, insistent drumming awakened me.

I rubbed my eyes, stretched. The noise came again, and I turned in that direction.

It was the window. Someone was rapping on the frame. I rose and crossed over, saw that it was Frank.

"Yeah?" I said. "What's up?"

"Come on out," he said. "It's important."

"Okay. Just a minute."

I went and rinsed my face, to complete the waking-up process and give me a chance to think. A glance at my watch showed me that it was around ten-thirty.

When I finally stepped outside, he seized my shoulder.

"Come on! Damn it! I told you it was important!"

I fell into step with him.

"All right! I had to wake up. What's the matter?"

"Paul's dead," he said.

"What?"

"You heard me. Dead."

"How'd it happen?"

"He stopped breathing."

"They usually do. But how did it happen?"

"I'd gotten to fooling with the unit you'd brought back. It's over there now. I moved it in when my time came to relieve Barthelme, so that I could keep working on it. Anyway, I got so involved that I wasn't paying much attention to him. When I finally did check on him again, he was dead. That's all. His face was dark and twisted. Some sort of lung failure, it seems. Maybe there was an air embolism. . . ."

We entered the rear of the building, the nearest entrance, the water splashing softly behind us, a light breeze following us in. We passed the recently set-up workbench, tools and the partly dismantled sonic unit spread across its surface. Rounding the corner to our left, we entered the room where Paul lay. I switched the light on.

His face was no longer handsome, bearing now the signs of one who had spent his final moments fighting for breath. I crossed to him, felt for a pulse, knew in advance I would find none. I covered a fingernail with my thumb and squeezed. It remained white when I released it.

"How long ago?" I asked.

"Right before I came for you."

"Why me?"

"You were nearest."

"I see. Was the sheet torn in this place before, I wonder?"

"I don't know."

"There were no cries, no sounds at all?"

"I didn't hear anything. If I had, I would have come right away."

I felt a sudden desire for a cigarette, but there were oxygen tanks in the room and NO SMOKING signs all over the building. I turned and retraced my steps, pushed the door open, held it with my back—leaning against it—lit a cigarette, and stared out across the water.

"Very neat," I said then. "With the day's symptoms behind him, he'll warrant a 'natural causes' with a 'possible air embolism,' 'congestive lung failure,' or some damn thing behind it."

"What do you mean?" Frank demanded.

"Was he sedated? I don't know. It doesn't matter. I'd imagine you used the recompressor. Right? Or did you tough it out and just smother him?"

"Come off it. Why would I—"

"In a way, I helped kill him," I said. "I thought he was safe with you here because you hadn't done anything about him all this time. You wanted to keep her, to win her back. Spending a lot of money on her was one way you tried. But it was a vicious circle, because Paul was a part of your source of extra revenue.

Then I came along and offered an alternative supply. Then today's accident, the whole setup here tonight . . . You rose to the occasion, seized the opportunity, and slammed the barn door. Not to mention striking while the iron was hot. Congratulations. I think you'll get away with it. Because this is all guesswork, of course. There is no real proof. Good show."

He sighed.

"Then why go into all that? It's over. We will go see Barthelme now and you will talk because I will be too distraught."

"But I'm curious about Rudy and Mike. I've been wondering all along. Did you have any part in it when they got theirs?"

"What do you know?" he asked slowly. "And how do you know it?"

"I know that Paul and Mike were the source of the stones. I know that Rudy found out and tried to blackmail them. They dealt with him, and I think Paul took care of Mike for good measure at the same time. How do I know? Paul babbled all the way back this afternoon and I was in the decompressor with him, remember? I learned about the diamonds, the murders, and about Linda and Paul, just by listening."

He leaned back against the workbench. He shook his head.

"I was suspicious of you," he said, "but you had the diamonds for proof. You came across them awfully fast, I'll admit. But I accepted your story because of the possibility that Paul's deposit was really somewhere quite near. He never told me where it was either. I decided you had to have either stumbled across it or followed him to it and known enough to recognize it for what it was. Whichever way, though, it doesn't matter. I would rather do business with you. Shall we just leave the whole thing at that?"

"If you will tell me about Rudy and Mike."

"I don't really know any more than what you've just said. That was none of my affair. Paul took care of everything. Answer one for me now: How did you find the deposit?"

"I didn't," I said. "I haven't the least idea where he got them."

He straightened.

"I don't believe you! The stones—where did they come from?"

"I found where Paul had hidden a bag of them. I stole it."

"Why?"

"Money, of course."

"Then why did you lie to me about where you got them?"

"You think I'd come out and say they were stolen? Now, though—"

He came forward very fast, and I saw that he had a large wrench in his hand.

I jumped backward, and the door caught him on the shoulder as it snapped inward. It only slowed him for an instant, though. He burst through and was at me again. I continued my retreat, falling into a defensive position.

He swung and I dodged to the side, chopping at his elbow. We both missed. His backstroke grazed my shoulder then, so that the blow I did land, seconds later, fell near his kidney with less force than I had hoped for. I danced back as he swung again, and my kick caught him on the hip. He dropped to one knee, but was up again before I could press in, swinging toward my head. I backed farther and he stalked me.

I could hear the water, smell it. I wondered about diving in. He was awfully close, though . . .

When he came in again, I twisted back and grabbed for his arm. I caught hold near the elbow and hung on, hooking my fingers toward his face. He drove himself into me then and I fell, still clutching his arm, catching hold of his belt with my other hand. My shoulder smashed against the ground, and he was on top of me, wrestling to free his arm. As he succeeded in dragging it away, his weight came off me for an instant. Pulling free, I doubled myself into a ball and kicked out with both legs.

They connected. I heard him grunt.

Then he was gone.

I heard him splashing about in the water. I also heard distant voices, calling, approaching us from across the islet.

I regained my feet. I moved toward the edge.

Then he screamed—a long, awful, agonized wail.

By the time I reached the edge, it had ceased.

When Barthelme came up beside me, he stopped repeating "What happened?" as soon as he looked down and saw the flashing fins at the center of the turmoil. Then he said, "Oh, my God!" And then nothing.

In my statement, later, I said that he had seemed highly agitated when he had come to get me, that he told me Paul had stopped breathing, that I had returned with him to the dispensary, determined that Paul was indeed dead, said so, and asked him for the details; that as we were talking he seemed to get the impression that I thought he had been negligent and somehow contributed to the death; that he had grown further agitated and finally attacked me; that we had fought and he had fallen into the water. All of which, of course, was correct. Deponent sinneth only by omission. They seemed to buy it. They went away. The shark hung around, waiting for dessert perhaps, and the dolphin people came and anesthetized him and took him away. Barthelme told me the damaged sonic projector could indeed have been shorting intermittently.

So Paul had killed Rudy and Mike; Frank had killed Paul and then been killed himself by the shark on whom the first two killings could now be blamed. The dolphins were cleared, and there was no one left to bring to justice for anything. The source of the diamonds was now one of life's numerous little mysteries.

. . . So, after everyone had departed, the statements been taken, the remains of the remains removed—long after that, as the night hung late, clear, clean, with its bright multitudes doubled in their pulsing within the cool flow of the Gulf Stream about the station, I sat in a deck chair on the small patio behind my quarters, drinking a can of beer and watching the stars go by.

. . . I needed but stamp CLOSED on my mental file.

But who had written me the note, the note that had set the infernal machine to chugging?

Did it really matter, now that the job was done? As long as they kept quiet about me . . .

I took another sip of beer.

Yes, it did, I decided. I might as well look around a bit more.

I withdrew a cigarette and moved to light it . . .

* * *

When I pulled into the harbor, the lights were on. As I climbed to the pier, her voice came to me over a loudspeaker.

She greeted me by name—my real name, which I hadn't heard spoken in a long while—and she asked me to come in.

I moved across the pier and up to the front of the building. The door stood ajar. I entered.

It was a long, low room, completely Oriental in decor. She wore a green silk kimono. She knelt on the floor, a tea service laid before her.

"Please come and be seated," she said.

I nodded, removed my shoes, crossed the room and sat down.

"*O-cha do desu-ka?*" she asked.

"*Itadakimasu.*"

She poured, and we sipped tea for a time. After the second cup I drew an ashtray toward me.

"Cigarette?" I asked.

"I don't smoke," she said. "But I wish you would. I try to take as few noxious substances into my own system as possible. I suppose that is how the whole thing began."

I lit one for me.

"I've never met a genuine telepath before," I said, "that I know of."

"I'd trade it for a sound body," she said, "any day. It wouldn't even have to be especially attractive."

"I don't suppose there is even a real need for me to ask my questions," I said.

"No," she said, "not really. How free do you think our wills might be?"

"Less every day," I said.

She smiled.

"I asked that," she said, "because I have thought a lot about it of late. I thought of a little girl I once knew, a girl who lived in a garden of terrible flowers. They were beautiful, and they were there to make her happy to look upon. But they could not hide their odor from her, and that was the odor of pity. For she was a sick little girl. So it was not their colors and textures from which she fled, but rather the fragrance which few knew she could detect. It was a painful thing to smell it constantly, and so in solitude she found her something of peace. Had it not been for her ability she would have remained in the garden."

She paused to take a sip of tea.

"One day she found friends," she continued, "in an unexpected place. The dolphin is a joyous fellow, his heart uncluttered with the pity that demeans. The way of knowing that had set her apart, had sent her away, here brought her close. She came to know the hearts, the thoughts of her new friends more perfectly than men know those of one another. She came to love them, to be one of their family."

She took another sip of tea, then sat in silence for a time, staring into the cup.

"There are great ones among them," she said finally, "such as you guessed at earlier. Prophet, seer, philosopher, musician—there is no man-made word I know of to describe this sort of one, or the function he performs. There are, however, those among them who voice the dreamsong with particular subtlety and profundity—something like music, yet not, drawn from that timeless place in themselves where perhaps they look upon the infinite, then phrase it for their fellows. The greatest I have ever known"—and she clicked the syllables in a high-pitched tone—"bears something like 'Kjwalll'kje'k'koothaïlll'kje'k for name or title. I could no more explain his dreamsong to you than I could explain Mozart to one who had never heard music. But when he, in his place, came to be threatened, I did what must be done."

"You see that I fail to see," I said, lowering my cup.

She refilled it, and then, "The Chickcharny is built up over the water," she said, and a vision of it came clear, disturbingly real, into my mind. "Like that," she said.

"I do not drink strong beverages, I do not smoke, I seldom

take medication," she said. "This is not a matter of choice. It is a physiological rule I break at my own peril. But should I not enjoy the same things others of my kind may know, just as I now enjoy the cigarette we are smoking?"

"I begin to see—"

"Swimming beneath the ashram at night, I could ride the mounting drug dreams of that place, know the peace, the happiness, the joy, and withdraw if it turned to something else—"

"Mike—" I said.

"Yes, it was he who led me to 'Kjwalll'kje'k'koothaïlll'kje'k, all unknowing. I saw there the place where they had found the diamonds. I see that you think it is near Martinique, since I was there just recently. I will not answer you on this. I saw there too, however, the idea of hurting dolphins. It seemed that they had been driven away from the place of their discovery—though not harmed—by dolphins. Several times. I found this so unusual that I was moved to investigate, and I learned that it was true. The place of their discovery was in the area of his song. He dwells in those waters, and others come to hear him there. It is, in this sense, a special place, because of his presence. They were seeking a way to ensure their own safety when they returned for more of the stones," she went on. "They learned of the effects of the noises of the killer whale for this purpose. But they also obtained explosives, should the recording prove insufficient over a period of days.

"The two killings occurred while I was away," she said. "You are essentially correct as to what was done. I had not known they would take place, nor would my telling of Paul's thoughts ever be admissible in any court. He used everything he ever got his hands or mind around, that man—however poor his grasp. He took Frank's theory as well as his wife, learned just enough to find the stones, with a little luck. Luck—he had that for a long while. He learned just enough about dolphins to know of the effects of the sounds of the killer whale, but not how they would behave if they had to fight, to kill. And even there he was lucky. The story was accepted. Not by everybody. But it was given sufficient credence. He was safe. And he planned to go back to—the place. I sought a way to stop him. And I wanted to see the dolphins vindicated—but that was of secondary importance, then. Then you appeared, and I knew that I had found it. I went to the station at night, crawled ashore, left you a note."

"And you damaged the sonic-broadcast unit?"

"Yes."

"You did it at such a time that you knew Paul and I would go down together to replace it."

"Yes."

"And the other?"

"Yes, that too. I filled Paul's mind with things I had felt and seen beneath the ashram of the Chickcharny."

"And you could look into Frank's mind as well. You knew how he would react. You set up the murder!"

"I did not force him to do anything. Is not his will as free as our own?"

I looked down into the tea, troubled by the thought. I gulped it. Then I stared at her.

"Did you not control him, even a little, near the end, when he attacked me? Or—far more important—what of a more rudimentary nervous system? Could you control the actions of a shark?"

She refilled my teacup.

"Of course not," she said.

We sat for another silent time. Then, "What did you try to do to me when I decided to continue my investigation?" I asked. "Were you not trying to baffle my senses and drive me to destruction?"

"No," she said quickly. "I was watching you to see what you would decide. You frightened me with your decision. But what I did was not an attack, at first. I tried to show you something of the dreamsong, to soothe you, to put you at peace. I had hoped that such an experience might work some mental alchemy, would soften your resolve—"

"You would have accompanied it with suggestions to that effect."

"Yes, I would have. But then you burned yourself and the pain pulled you back. That was when I attacked you."

She suddenly sounded tired. But then, it had been a very busy day for her, all things considered.

"And this was my mistake," she said. "Had I simply let you go on, you would have had nothing. But you saw the unnatural nature of the attack. You associated it with Paul's raptures, and you thought of me—a mutant—and of dolphins and diamonds and my recent trip. It all spilled into your mind—and then the threat that I saw you could keep: alluvial diamonds and Martinique, into the central data bank. I had to call you then, to talk."

"What now?" I asked. "No court could ever convict you of anything. You are safe. *I* can hardly condemn you. My own hands are not free of blood, as you must know. You are the only person alive who knows who I am, and that makes me uncomfortable. Yet I have some guesses concerning things you would not like known. You will not try to destroy me, for you know what I will do with these guesses if you fail."

"And I see that you will not use your ring unless you are provoked. Thank you. I have feared it."

"It appears that we have reached something of a standoff."

"Then why do we not both forget?"

"You mean—trust each other?"

"Is it so novel a thing?"

"You must admit you are possessed of a small edge in such matters."

"True. But it is of value only for the moment. People change. It does not show me what you will be thinking on another day, in some other place. You are in a better position to know that, for you have known yourself far longer than I."

"True, I suppose."

"I, of course, really have nothing to gain by destroying the pattern of your existence. You, on the other hand, could conceivably be moved to seek an unrecorded source of income."

"I can't deny that," I said. "But if I gave you my word, I would keep it."

"I know that you mean that. I also know that you believe much of what I have said, with some reservations."

I nodded.

"You do not really understand the significance of 'Kjwalll'kje'k'koothaïlll'kje'k."

"How could I, not being a dolphin or even a telepath?"

"May I show you what it is that I am seeking to preserve, to defend?"

I thought about it for a time, recalling those recent moments back at the station when she had hit me with something out of William James. I had no way of knowing what manner of control, what sort of powers she might be able to exercise upon me if I agreed to some experiment along these lines. However, if things got out of control, if there was the least feeling of meddling with my mind, beyond the thing itself, I knew a way to terminate the experience instantly. I folded my hands before me, laying two fingers upon my ring.

"Very well," I said.

And then it began again, something like music, yet not, some development of a proposition that could not be verbalized, for its substance was of a stuff that no man possessed or perceived, lying outside the range of human sensory equipment. I realized then that that part of me which experienced this had its place temporarily in the mind of the statement's creator, that this was the dreamsong of 'Kjwalll'kje'k'koothaïlll'kje'k, that I witnessed/participated in the timeless argument as he improvised, orchestrated it, drawing entire sections of previously constructed visions and phrasings, perfect and pure, from a memory so vital that its workings were barely distinguishable from the activities of the moment, and blending these into fresh harmonies to a joyous rhythm I comprehended only obliquely, through the simultaneous sensing of his own pleasure in the act of their formulation.

I felt the delight in this dance of thought, rational though not logical: the process, like all of art, was an answer to something, though precisely what, I did not know nor really care; for it was, in and of itself, a sufficiency of being—and if one day it were to provide me with an emotional weapon at a time when I would otherwise stand naked and alone, why this was one of the things none has the right to expect, yet sometimes discovers within the recollection of such fragments of existence cast by a special seer with a kind of furious joy.

I forgot my own being, abandoned my limited range of senses as I swam in a sea that was neither dark nor light, formed nor formless, yet knowing my way, subsumed, as it were, within a perpetual act of that thing we had decided to call *ludus* that was creation, destruction, and sustenance, patterned and infinitely repatterned, scattered and joined, mounting and descending, divorced from all temporal phenomena yet containing the essence of time. Time's soul it seemed I was, the infinite potentialities that fill the moment, surrounding and infusing the tiny stream of existence, and joyous, joyous, joyous . . .

Spinning, my mind came away, and I sat, still clutching my death ring, across from the little girl who had fled from the terrible flowers, now clad in wet green and very, very wan.

"*O-cha do desu-ka?*" she asked.

"*Itadakimasu.*"

She poured. I wanted to reach out and touch her hand, but I raised the teacup instead and sipped from it.

She had my answer, of course. She knew.

But she spoke, after a time: "When my moment comes—who knows how soon?—I shall go to him," she said. "I shall be there, with 'Kjwalll'kje'k'koothaïlll'kje'k. Who knows but that I shall continue, as a memory perhaps, in that timeless place, as a part of the dreamsong? But then, I feel a part of it now."

"I—"

She raised her hand. We finished our tea in silence.

I did not really want to go then, but I knew that I must.

There were so many things that I might have said, I thought, as I headed the *Isabella* back toward Station One, my bag of diamonds, and all the other things and people I had left behind, waiting for me to touch them or speak to them.

But then, I reflected, the best words are often those left unsaid.

MY BROTHER LEOPOLD

Edgar Pangborn

§1

Memorandum from Jermyn Graz, Frater Literatus & Precentor, to His Beneficence Alesandar Fitzeral, O.S.S., Abbot of St. Benjamin's at Mount Orlook in the Province of Ulsta, November 21, 465.

My dear Lord Abbot:

Your Beneficence has graciously requested information in writing concerning the life of my brother Leopold Graz, thirty-eight years deceased, for the attention of the Examiners from the Holy City when they determine his spiritual status, whether the Church shall declare him beatified. My days of delay have been spent in prayer, wondering how best to comply. In spite of time, my brother's death is new to me as yesterday; I am troubled and uncertain.

For longer than I wish to recall, I have been more an observer than a participant in the sorrowful comedy. I will try to write a narrative as simple as the rings of a tree trunk. I have lived a long time, as my brother Leopold did not, since we played together as boys with Jon Rohan and Sidney Sturm, the four of us a natural company, ever loyal (we thought)—one for all and all (we thought) for one. I think I would have died for any of them, certainly for Sidney, as we swore our readiness to do one day when Jon snagged his pinkie on a thorn and we hurried to make use of the fine fresh gore for writing purposes. Oh, how long ago!—I am bald and slow and wrinkled, and tonight my joints pain me.

I have made the common pilgrimages—to Filadelfia, Albani, the shrines of Conicut and Levannon. I never made the long pilgrimage in Abraham's footsteps to the Old City of Nuin on the Atlantic, but I saw that ocean once, when I traveled as a young man to the highland from which one sees the Black Rocks emerge at low tide like scarecrows in the mouth of the Hudson Sea, and beyond them the great waters. I have beheld other marvels, including adult loyalties that warmed me—but I don't find these more intense than those of boyhood, or less frail; seldom as joyous, since adult loyalties may be stained by cynicism, weariness, second thoughts.

I have been for fifteen years precentor here under your tranquil rule. You will remember I was a monk, inscribing after my name the good letters O.S.S.,* long before that. I am also proud of my secular name Jermyn Graz, for our artisan father came from an agrarian family descended from a commune of Old Time; yet I am content to be only your devoted Fr. Jermyn, precentor of this Abbey.

My brother Leopold was born December 13, 405. Thirty-eight years ago, in the reign of Emperor Mahonn and the patriarchate of Urbanus II, he was arrested under the name of Brother Francis, charged with treason, and transferred after ten months' imprisonment to the Ecclesiastical Court at Nuber on suspicion of heresy. And as you know, he was tried, condemned, and executed at Kingstone, October 28, 427.

I have never had the privilege of reading the trial transcript,

* *Ordo Sancti Silvani.*

but my memory lives. When they bound him to the stake the sky did darken and a torrent flooded the streets; the soldiers were obliged to pour oil on the faggots. Some murmured that this showed disregard for God's voice in the storm, but then the crowd fought in the usual way, trampling and shoving to snatch magic relics from the ashes.

None of our family survives him but myself. Our father died years before Leopold's execution, and our mother still longer ago, when Leo was seven. I think the Examiners may disregard the rambling of my mother's sister Lora Stone, who thinks my mother had had no carnal knowledge of our father Louis Graz in the nine months before Leopold's birth, but was impregnated by fire from heaven. My aunt is very old, fumbling at the past like a child with broken playthings. She did not come to live with us until a year after my mother died.

We are taught that none can be born without sin; that every birth delays the Liquidation, our destiny. But sometimes I sinfully wish I might have held in my arms a child of my brother Leopold.

And I am ravaged by doubts, my Lord Abbot, especially on summer nights after Matins when I should be attentive at prayer. I fall to imagining this earth not liquidated but inhabited by a people changed, no longer constantly at war nor obsessed by greed and fear, a people such as my brother spoke of as dwelling in a City of Light. They would deal charitably; they would enjoy their days. They might one day recapture the lost skill of Old Time and journey to the stars—but then I recall how little can be left of the resources of earth that made this conceivable in Old Time, and I am back in the old cobwebbed halls of human folly without a candle. I have never mentioned these doubts in confession; I have hugged the small sin to myself for comfort, until now this question of my brother's sainthood has smoked me out. The study of history (under Church guidance) has been my life. I am forced to see Old Time as an age when men, by their own written admission, had so wasted and befouled the earth that it could no longer support their fearsome numbers, and nature cut them down with war, plague, famine, and that bearing of sterile monsters which follows intercourse like a tax paid to Hell. And still I persist in wondering whether folly must always be our nemesis. To me the beauty of earth, of its other dwellers less arrogant than man, often appears more sublime than our grandest achievements. Where nature spreads a floor of loveliness we scrape our feet and shit on it.

[*In the brittle faded original of this letter by Jermyn Graz the foregoing paragraph is marked by a marginal line and exclamation point, probably conveying indignation. This mark was undoubtedly made by* Wilmot Breen, *a justice of the Ecclesia and the ranking prelate of the* Nuber Examiners *in 465, for his initials in the same script and ink are attached to other marginal notes further on.*]

I know we are taught that in a few years the elect shall be taken into heaven and all others submerged as if they had never been, when the oceans rise entirely above the dry land, and the world as we have known it passes away, a drop of water in the firmament. Still, when the nights are in summer and I hear the sad-merry clash of the crickets and katydids and trill of frogs in the moist woods beyond the monastery walls—my lord, I wonder and I wonder.

I alone live to remember Leopold as a child. Jon Rohan died in 435 from aftereffects of a wound received in the War of 426-429. I lost Sidney before that: a devoted young doctor, he died in 430, the year of the red plague that followed the Moha War —a return, some say, of the epidemic that did so much to destroy the society of Old Time. I alone recall the voice of the boy Leopold in the choir of the Kingstone Cathedral, how it soared.

Here was a day of 413: Leopold seven, I fourteen, Jon Rohan twelve, Sidney fifteen. We met a black-browed Gypsy, old and horny-footed, in a meadow by Twenyet Road; we were wandering, not far from home.

We had been trained to fear and avoid Gypsies, as children are usually guarded against any strangeness that might illuminate the strangeness within themselves. We saw a sagging wagon in the meadow, a crowbait tethered on succulent grass, and would have slipped past. Something of mirage or phantasm was in the heaviness of the afternoon. It was that pregnant month, July. Before we saw the wagon, Leopold had been singing for us, casually; we had noticed a hawk high in the blue.

The Gypsy sat motionless on the gray stump of a tree beside the road, wearing a dull loin-rag and colorless sandals. His knotty flesh was brown like the earth behind him, his gray hair speckled white like the quills of a porcupine. He had a shoulder satchel; a clay pipe dangled in his hand unlit. I smelled sweat and coarse Conicut tobacco.

I am not fey. I was born for the prosaic life, passions and marvels passing me as a parade might wind down the road past a child who cannot open the window and call. But I have a more than natural sense for stress and change in others. I knew Jon was startled by the Gypsy and hostile. Sidney was startled too, but pleasantly, the sweetness of his nature responding to anything that showed no enmity. I knew my brother Leopold felt a recognition outside my understanding, as if in some territory out of time where he and the grizzled Gypsy could meet as contemporaries with a shared language.

The Gypsy asked: "Would any of you gentlemen possess a tinderbox? Mine's in my wagon and I too lazy to go stumping after it."

I had a fine new one, a present from my father. Up I stepped, and when the old man had tamped in fresh tobacco I made a light for him, my sliver of flame stabbing down into the gurgling bowl. Sidney stood near, and I knew his thought was for my safety, but the Gypsy was smiling with all dusty wrinkles. "I thank you."

I said as I'd been taught: "It's nothing—you're welcome."

"Welcome—that's a variety of love, ain't it?"

His question seemed directed at Sidney, the oldest of us, the kind one, slim and golden in the sun. Sidney smiled. Jon was standing apart and frowning, working his toes in the dust.

"So everything comes from nothing," said the Gypsy, "and that's what makes the world go round? Am I right, Youngest?" This to Leopold, who had ducked in under my arm. Either Leopold nodded or the Gypsy pretended he had. "I'm right," he said, puffing, "and it's not a bad arrangement, for if the world quit going round wouldn't we fly off like beads from the end of a busted string?" Then he lifted some articles from his satchel and displayed them in the palm of his left hand. "Anyhow, I suppose I'm among gentlemen who believe the world is round. True, Youngest?"

My little brother said: "My name's Leopold."

"Why, that's a sensible answer." Then the Gypsy's gaze was piercing me. "My Ma named me Aleites. You'll be Leopold's brother." Seldom did others notice a resemblance. In those days I was sandy blond; Leopold's hair was dark as walnut. Our other features differed: Leopold had a straight nose, a glorious high arch of brow; my nose was alway puggy, my lips too full. But that Gypsy saw our brotherhood. "And the name people call you—?"

"Jermyn."

"Light and welcome—I must make you a return." He was moving his big right hand over his left, jumbling the oddments there like one preparing a throw of the dice. "Jermyn, I'd have you choose one from this lot—alas, worthless as men measure things in the marketplace. Choose something to please all your blithe company." I stared at his palm, incapable of decision; it looked big as a plowed field. "Here, for instance, my dear, is a bit of a garnet—I don't claim it gives the wearer invisibility; we're sensible people, aren't we? Here's the milk tooth of a chimera, which some say confers bravery if worn next the skin—*I* don't say it, of course. And this gold phallus no bigger'n a thumbnail—perky, ain't it? Made for a king's son likely, the way every wench he met in his travels was *supposed* to jump out of her skin to please him, since we all know that next to a big one they like a gold one; but I never tried it out, don't actually know a thing about it. I never guarantee a blessed thing; that's why I'm a successful businessman." His old nag nickered at that, and he had the grace to look embarrassed.

I grew desperate. I thought Jon might like the chimera's milk tooth; he was always for games that tested our company's bravery, maybe from a need in himself to prove he was brave enough to meet the world head-on. Jon's father was a captain of engineers in the 2nd Ulsta Regiment, a loud, urgent man. I would have done anything to please Sidney, but couldn't imagine what he might like out of that jumble. Then I saw how my brother's eyes yearned at one thing there, a thing the Gypsy hadn't even mentioned.

This was a lump of clay no longer than my thumb, a trifle stouter, so worn by time you needed a second look to understand it was sculpture, the stylized figure of a little human male with arms folded against his chest, hands flat to the body. And on the other side of the lump—the Gypsy turned it over for me—was a woman's figure sharing the clay body, her face brooding like the man's and mild. I glanced again at Leopold, touched the image, said: "That."

The Gypsy gave me the dingy thing and dribbled the other objects back into his bag. Oh, the glitter of them, the gleam of what I might have had! "You've made the strange choice," he said. "Heaven knows what will come of it, or maybe Heaven doesn't know."

"That's heresy," said Jon Rohan.

"It's heresy," said the Gypsy, "or it's an outlander's way of talking, meaning no harm. Pipe's out—back to work. Bless you and good morning to you, gentlemen." He shambled off to his wagon, and we four straggled back home with our thoughts.

Leopold asked: "Maybe I can keep it for you?" So I gave him the image, wishing it were any of a thousand better things.

Many times since then I have held the image before me, and it has taken me into contemplation; then I am like one caught up to the arch of heaven with no company but the falling stars. In his own fashion my brother must have responded for a while to this same power of the clay. I remember how lovingly he first dropped it into the pocket of his blouse and held a protective hand over it, as another child might cherish a pet. It was only a little later that I began hearing about Leopold's Companion, concerning whose existence the Church Examiners, I suppose, will wish more light.

My brother shared the bed with me in our attic room, a dear fidgeting nuisance. Our mother loved him best: this I had always known as children do know it. But the years that brought him out of babyhood carried her into exhaustion and invalidism, no strength left for contending with small boys. Losing her in these dim ways, we found each other. By the time Leopold was five I think my jealousy had dissolved in fondness, answering his natural warmth. Whether darker feelings still smoldered I cannot say—it was long ago.

The night after our meeting with the Gypsy, Leopold bounced under the covers holding the image, lost it during sleep, went frantic hunting for it in the morning. When we salvaged it from the bedclothes, he put it on a string to wear at his neck—not good, for the image was worn so smooth it had hardly a projection for the cord to hold. For Leopold's eighth birthday, Jon and Sidney and I collaborated on a solution. Sidney, brilliant with his hands, carved a box of applewood with a secret fastening; Jon bought a delicate silver chain in an antiquity shop—it cost him two months' allowance—and I joined the chain to the box in my father's workshop. Leopold was speechless with joy, opening and shutting the mysterious catch forty times a day. I have the box still, and the image secure in its nest that Sidney made, his magic as good as ever after half a century.

Our mother was going through a cruel pregnancy. Her time came on her not long after the day we met the Gypsy. For several weeks her illness had brought Leopold and me more than ever together; but there were times when he seemed utterly alone, in unchildlike contemplation of the image. Silent in a corner of the cobbler shop, he could have been on the other side of the stars.

Our house was one of the many shabby-genteel ones that cluster along the Twenyet Road in Kingstone. The Old Time city of the same name stood southeast of there, now mostly underwater of course. We lived about three miles from Rondo's Shrine, where the Old Time course of the Twenyet Road takes it under Lake Ashoka. The modern detour curves over higher ground to meet the old road emerging. In many places one still finds the gray rubbish, curious Old Time road material, frost-heaved, pried loose, dumped out of the way. This work of clearance and improvement was done, I believe, more than a hundred years ago in the era of construction after Katskil became an Empire.* Farther out in the country, much of the gray junk has been hauled off by farmers to add to their stone fences. A great deal more of the repulsive indestructible garbage of Old Time might be put to some use, if we would exercise more ingenuity.

Our section of the Twenyet Road was called The Crafts, because so many artisans lived there to catch the trade of travelers entering the city. Father was a shoemaker, dark-gloomy like the tanned hides he labored with, strict with Leopold and me in matters of decorum and truthtelling, but strict with justice and not unkind. He was one of those who fend off love with a grunt and then admit it anyway.

Our mother was soft, no disciplinarian. She enjoyed those romances the Church approves for the common people, for unlike our father she had learned to read, at a wise woman's school in her native village; sometimes housework waited while she dwelt in a storyteller's daydream—who could begrudge it to her? Between my birth and Leo's she had borne two mues. It was at her insistence that Father sent me to Mam Sola's day school in Kingstone, where I met Sidney and learned my letters and arithmetic. I have always been grateful for it: a little reading may prove a key to great reading. I cannot help thinking, my Lord Abbot, that a fairly widespread literacy might usefully supplement our Imperial Program of Universal Education.

I know nothing about those other two mues. This late pregnancy our mother was suffering was terminated by the birth of a monster, a twelve-pound hulk of flesh with four arms and, the priest told me later, no anus. He had quickly smothered the thing as the law requires, and it must have been buried quickly too, in the dark and without any ceremony, as is proper, in that sad tombless yard—Mues' Acre—that every church must maintain beyond the limits of its natural cemetery. But while Fr. Colin disposed of it, the midwife could not prevent our mother from bleeding to death.

*Cf. *Harker Sidon,* Old-Time Survivals in Imperial Katskil, *Filadelfia College Press, 748. But Professor Sidon is mainly concerned with the physical survivals; one must look elsewhere for discussion of the mental inheritance.*

During this ordeal I was in the attic room charged with keeping Leopold out of the way. He was beside himself when the screaming began, though he heard my explanations. I held him fast and said over and over: "They're trying to help her." His heart hammered and his eyes were blind. We heard a last scream, beyond bearing, a flurry of voices, quick footsteps, orders. I must have relaxed my grip, for Leopold tore free and rushed downstairs. I caught up with him in the kitchen. Fr. Colin, that sardonic old man who always befriended me, was wrapping the thing in a cloth, but did not get it out of sight swiftly enough. Leopold saw it, and collapsed.

"Get him outside, Jermyn," said Fr. Colin. "Fresh air will bring him back to this delightful world." I carried him out into the moonlit splendor of a field behind our house. I kissed him and talked to him. He roused when I moved the locket with the clay image because it was making a hurting hardness between him and me. His eyes opened; he was back with me, gripping the amulet as if it were a bridge to life. "It's all right," I said. "It's all right, Leo." We both knew it was all wrong. Leo at eight understood how our human talk uses these flat reversals of reason. "Happens all the time—the priest says it's the will of God because men were so wicked in Old Time." I went on till I ran out of respectable words.

His night eyes watched me. He took the image from its box and studied it in the white light, turning it from male to female side and back. "Jermyn, why can't people make babies the way grapevines do?" Startled, I laughed. "You might've rested a part of you on the ground till I grew out of it and it was time to cut me free." He knew he was talking absurdly. He said: "I'll preach when I grow up."

"Well, sure. Mother's always wanted you to be a priest."

"No, I won't be a priest. But I'll preach. I'll say it about the grapevines. It's a—a—" Maybe he wanted to say "parable" and didn't have the word. "And I'll tell about the City of Light. The Companion will teach me how."

"The Companion?"

"He came yesterday when I looked at Two-Face. He stands

where light and dark come together." He watched me as if he longed to explain further and could not. It was no playacting. We were too close for that, in spite of the seven years; when any playacting was to be done, we shared it.

I said: "Tell me about him. Please. What does he look like?"

"Not always the same. Only a voice sometimes."

I was frightened, and lacerated by jealousy. I saw this Companion taking Leopold away—as perhaps he did, even if we grant him existence only in my brother's mind. I asked: "What is the City of Light?"

"A place the Companion knows." He said no more, but he was not trying to mystify me.

In the house, Fr. Colin told us our mother was dead. "Try to be good boys to your father," he said, fumbling at the unsayable.

Leopold asked like a grown-up: "Is he with her now?"

"Yes," he said. "Take them in, Sister Alma." The midwife was fluttering, poor-boying us, another of the well-meaning ones. She took us where our father sat stricken beside that little dark lady once so well known, now gone secret, the blanket pulled to her chin and she with no more regard for anyone, not even Father. Fr. Colin said: "Leo, you'll understand better when you come to be a priest yourself. God has His reasons, child—it's only that we can't always know them."

But Leopold said: "I cannot be a priest."

Father lifted his head. "Leopold, what do you mean?"

"I can't be a priest." He said this, standing by our mother's body. I remember putting an arm around him because I feared the grown-up world was about to roar at him.

But no. Fr. Colin mumbled about our mother's wish that he might enter holy orders. I scarcely heard that, waiting for what Father would say. It was a gentle reply: "Of course, Leo, you can't be a priest unless you wish it yourself. We'll talk of it later."

But so far as I know it was never brought up again. From that time on, however—the Examiners may find this important—Leopold was intensely keen to share whatever knowledge I brought home from Mam Sola's school. He took to reading like a baby fish to swimming. He gulped down all I could transmit, with impatience for its simplicity, begging for more difficult tasks. "Where are the big books?" he'd demand of me. "*Where are the books?*"

I was not a bad student, indeed Mam Sola praised me, but beside Leo I was a stumbling mule. Two years after our mother's death I resolved to work full time in Father's shop, while Leo would attend the school in my place, but soon he reported that Mam Sola said he knew all she could teach him. She wanted him to go to the great Priests' School at Nuber, and this she and Father arranged for him, beginning in the winter of 415–416, when he was ten. He was the baby of his class among yeasty adolescents; luckily, some of them made a pet of him, sheltering him from the mindless cruelties the majority would have visited on him if they had dared. The priests loved him too after their fashion, seeing maybe a future Patriarch, who knows?

The years 412–418—being nearly my contemporary, my Lord Abbot, Your Beneficence will remember this fragment of time much as I do, and the gradual increase of hatred in our nation toward the Republic of Moha after the accession of the Emperor Mahonn. There was the Sortees Massacre, when Moha traders were set upon by a hysterical crowd—that might have brought war, but neither side was ready. There was the complaint that Moha was cutting us off from trade with Nuin—and nothing ever said about our monopoly of trade with the tropical wealth of Penn, the spices and tea and oranges. The Emperor Mahonn's accession brought a relief from uncertainty: now at least we all knew there would be war, and only the timing was unpredictable.

Those were also the six years when my brother grew from seven to thirteen, from jungle of childhood to river's edge.

Jon and Sidney and I found it natural that a small boy should believe in an invisible Companion: a common fantasy. I may have had such a dream myself before Leo was born. That it should continue beyond early childhood was not so natural—but we were credulous, ignorant boys, and in our different ways we too believed in the Companion's existence. We'd catch Leopold with the clay image in his hand, sunlight on his closed eyelids, listening, and we believed.

My lord, he spoke once of "my brother the sun." Now, it was not till many years later, in my historical studies, that I learned of a saint in ancient Christian times who used these words, and certainly before he went to the Nuber school my little brother had never heard of him; yet he did so speak.

We would keep watch for him, a sharp eye against intruders. Unless he himself was a-mind to discuss them, we never asked about those silent conversations. Had others learned of the mystery and bothered Leo, we would have gone after them like wildcats. Leopold had become to us an oracle, our mascot. After he began study at the Priests' School we had him only in the summers, but schoolboys live for that time anyhow. He was ours and he could do no wrong.

We fell into the habit of consulting him as if he possessed a magical insight; maybe he did. We would ask questions about whatever disturbed us—sex, making a living, religion, right and wrong conduct, superstitions—matters that lay far beyond the experience of his years (beyond ours too!). We would mull over his answers for nuggets of gold.

At that time I was not well instructed in the faith. Fr. Colin was swamped in the busyness of a parish priest's duties, his time for meditation and teaching chewed to bits by the million tiny mouths of everyday trivia. Our father was none too devout, and what early instruction we had from our mother had blended religion and romance in one blur of wishful dreaming. Father resented the tithes, the spending of time on devotion. During those six years, arthritis twisted his cobbler's hands; at times I heard him growl heretical complaints.

Jon Rohan, that chubby hero, was somewhat disciplined in religion. Sidney was agnostic, which frightened me, though he was always discreet—I would not say it now of my friend if he were not long dead, beyond reach of wounding. Later, deep in the humanitarian work of his choice, it seemed to me he was not concerning himself as much as he ought to have done with the safety of his soul; but good works, I am sure, have won him a place in Heaven, if Heaven exists.* It was not until after his death that I, adrift and wretched from the loss of him and of Leopold, took lay orders as a student of history, leading to my later work as a churchman. At the young time I am describing I had what I will call an undisciplined openness of mind. I found no heresy in believing my brother might converse with an angel.

I will write of an afternoon in early September in Leopold's thirteenth year when we had gone to a favorite clearing above the road to Maplestock. That forest belonged to the Ashoka family, long masters of the Maplestock region. Baron Ashoka's game wardens could legally have lobbed arrows into us on suspicion of poaching—shooting, of course, to cripple and not to kill.

I was twenty that September. Expert in my father's trade, I supposed I would remain a shoemaker. I already managed our shop: pain in the joints was making it nearly impossible for our stubborn old father to go on working. My aunt Mam Lora had kept house for us about five years now, her conversation all sniff and glare, making a cult of our mother as a martyred saint.

That afternoon was a Friday. In the morning we had gone to church, taking the rest of the day for a holiday as our customs then permitted. (My lord, I do dislike the modern trend toward a completely joyless Sabbath.) Sidney was returning soon to the University at Nuber for his third year of medical study. On the journey he would be looking after Leopold, who was going back for his last year at the Priests' School—then the University for him too, we assumed, since he was certain to be granted a scholarship. And Jon too was leaving, for the Military Academy at Nupal. I would stay home and make shoes.

Jon had said goodbye to his sweetheart, Sara Jonas, in the grandeur of his Academy uniform; he told us about that parting, modestly. Sara owned a great share of him, a delicious girl pretty as a violet in the snow. We found that right for one of Jon's temperament, but his humor and good nature appeared

* *In the margin, a note with the initials* W.B.: *"These are strange remarks for a precentor of your Abbey."*

to be jelling into a kind of sentimentality that made him no longer quite one of us. He in turn felt, I think, that he had outgrown us and was at eighteen the only adult in a gaggle of starry-eyed goslings. He took a deep melancholy joy in the war talk. He was like a prince condescending: let us pursue our mundane plans; for him, the lonely glory of going forth to die in our defense, thinking of Sara in his last hour. Not that he ever spoke such corn as that, yet we felt something of the sort in him. My own discomfort at his swashbuckling may have been partly envy: what has a shoemaker to do with war? Well, he makes boots for soldiers to march in, for soldiers to die in.

This was 418, eight years before the war actually began. When it did come, Jon was a captain of infantry, blooded during the Slaves' Rebellion in the western provinces (fomented by Moha, some claimed) in 422. And when the last great struggle with Moha did begin, our Jon was in the thick of it. He was wounded in action, suffering the loss of his left leg from the infection of a spear wound, and the blinding of his right eye. He came back thus to goodwife Sara and his small children: halt, half-blind, the infection still burning in the stump of the thighbone and never quite healing, an old man in his middle twenties. This ruin came on him in our defeat at Brakabin Meadows, April 4, 427, which brought the Moha forces within a short march of Kingstone. No one then could have imagined our recovery, our victories of the following year; 427 was ebb tide, all Katskil breathing despair. For his bravery at Brakabin, Jon received a life's pension and the Iron Wheel of the Order of St. Franklin.

I have digressed again, my lord—forgive me.

A September afternoon of 418, and Leopold had not sung for us that day. At thirteen his voice had cracked; the Cathedral choirmaster warned him not to sing again for two years. We missed it. Entertainments were few. We had the huge sermons of Fridays and Lecture Days; the street-corner storytellers, the peep shows, visits from Rambler caravans that ignored national boundaries and carried amusement, news, messages everywhere; that was about all. We found it hard to lose the pleasure of Leopold's singing and know it would never happen again as it had been, since Leo singing with a man's voice would be another happening in another world.

We bathed in a pool and dried ourselves in the sun. Leopold was not used to the new curly hair on him or the breaking of his voice, but didn't mind our jokes and bawdy counsel. We found it strange to watch the Mascot enter adolescence as we were emerging from it. His body was becoming like ours; his mind occupied other dimensions.

Jon asked: "Leo, what does the Companion say about the war?"

Leopold had lately spoken of the Companion only enough to let us know the conversations had not ended. He said: "Not much, Jon. A war will come sometime, and make an end of—many things."

"Why," said Jon, "everybody knows that."

Sidney inquired: "Because there always has been war?"

"It's a reason," said Jon. "You can't change human nature."

"But it does change," I asserted. "The history books—"

Jon wanted to argue with Sidney, not to hear about history. "It's the *cause*, Sid. The future belongs to Katskil. How can we make progress with Moha like a log across the road?"

(And since then I have read much history of Old Time, and of ancient time, and how often have I stumbled over these same worn words! Including my own protests, and Sidney's.)

"The future doesn't exist," Sidney said.

I put in: "Only in the mind of God."

"Progress by smashing skulls," said Sidney. "Destiny. Shit."

And Leopold: "Mue-births are bad enough, without war." Perhaps the Examiners ought to know that from our mother's death to the time I lost him, Leopold was obsessed with the tragedy of mue-births. Moments came now and then when his fresh and healthy child's face incredibly foreshadowed maturity, even old age—I don't think I imagined this; and when I saw it I could be almost certain what trouble it was that darkened him.

"No use being a bleeding-heart," Jon said. "Face facts!"

Sidney wouldn't get angry, even at that noise. "The facts stare me in the face, Jon, and I say there isn't one stupid thing between us and Moha that couldn't be settled at a conference table."

"But how can you trust 'em?"

Leopold said: "You're not hearing each other . . ."

Later Jon asked about the Companion. "Do you still—*see* him?"

"As if my eyes were shut, and I knowing the shape in memory. He speaks, and it's like a memory of hearing."

"Then it's only thinking? Imagining?"

"Maybe. He startles me, and then later I understand." Leopold frowned. "He described the City of Light like—a real place."

Sidney asked: "Do you believe in his separate existence, Leo, the way you believe I'm sitting here bare-ass and beautiful?"

"Not that way. But I think there is a City of Light."

That day was forty-seven years ago. After he left with Sidney for Nuber, I did not see my brother Leopold again for eight years.

We had a letter from him in November. I recall our heady excitement when the Imperial Post rider banged on our door. Letters came rarely to poor districts like Twenyet Road; Leo was being extravagant, undertaking such an expense just to send us greetings. We shut out the urchins who had gathered to stare at the rider, and then my father was beside himself with impatience till I could read him the message. However, that letter was one any schoolboy might have written to content his family: he was well, studying hard, sorry he couldn't be home for Thanksgiving but looked forward to seeing us in the Week of Abraham,* love to everybody.

In early December came a letter from Sidney: Leopold was gone.

* *All nations of eastern Murca in the Fifth Century professed Brownism, celebrating the supposed birth of Abraham Brown on December 24 and making the whole week a festival: an obvious superimposition on the Old Time Christmas. Brownism preferred mild methods of substitution and engulfment in its suppression of Christianity—one could almost speak of syncretism rather than suppression. The modern scholar is often puzzled to distinguish the newcomer from the ghost.*

On the night of December 7, Leopold had gone to bed as usual in the Senior Dormitory—thirty-six boys in a long room where all-night candles burned and a priest sat wakeful to suppress giggling and other unseemliness. In the morning, Leopold was not there.

The monitor priest admitted he could have dozed off. The other boys under severest questioning confessed no knowledge, and I think they had none. Leopold must simply have dressed himself silently and walked out. The night watchman spent his hours mostly at the gatehouse; Leo must have climbed the Pine Street wall, hidden by evergreens.

Sidney had not seen Leopold for two weeks before the disappearance; nothing then had seemed to Sidney unusual.

When I read this letter to my father, he gasped and fell—his first stroke. I got word of this to Sidney and Jon. Jon was not given leave of absence; Sidney left Nuber at once and reached our house by evening on a fast horse. In his embrace I found the relief of tears, till then denied. And Sidney gave me the clay image with its applewood box and silver chain. "He *left it behind,* Jermyn. Under his pillow." This we never did understand; nor do I, altogether, in later years. But so the amulet did return to me, my lord, and it has not since left my possession.

Sidney helped me untiringly in caring for my father, who was always asking for news of Leopold, we understood, with his eyes and the one finger he could move. Then soon, mercifully, he had another stroke, and died. We watched the difficult life recede, leaving the shell of our good cobbler Louis Graz, my father, and Sidney closed his eyes for me with his steadfast kindness.

For eight years, no word. Soon after my father's death my Aunt Lora entered the nunnery of St. Ellen at Nupal, where she is now in her ninety-fifth year. Sidney returned to the University, was graduated with high honors, finished his licentiate in 422, and started practice in Kingstone. That was also the year of the Slaves' Rebellion in which Jon Rohan rose to the rank of captain. I sold our house and cobbler shop—another of the gray milestones that emerge in anyone's life story. The buyer was well known to me; he would have notified me if Leopold had ever returned to that house. With a donkey and my cobbler's equipment, I took to the roads.

I had not lost my passion for reading and history. But it was in some manner reinforcing my grief at the loss of Leopold. There can be a weariness, even acedia, in too much history. I wished to escape it for a while. History repeats much of its sorrow, error, lost opportunity. Though I had learned a great deal about the folly and corruption of Old Time, I found small consolation in comparing past with present—I can't see that we have learned much from that dark story. In my monastic years I have collected, edited, sometimes rewritten legends and true tales of our region, past and present. This labor also, though congenial, has done little to alter my view. Hope is a lost child stumbling across a battlefield.

I had stronger reasons for a wanderer's life. An artisan may follow the roads: people must have shoes in a country of thorns and serpents. A peddler-artisan may listen. (Our Gypsy by the roadside was listening.) If careful not to startle or offend, he may ask some questions. I would not believe my brother Leopold was dead.

Sidney never discouraged my search. Jon thought Leo must be dead or carried off by slavers, and scolded me for wasting myself. Sidney aided me, his fine house at Kingstone my home whenever I wished. We knew Leopold, thirteen, harmless, could have had no enemies, and he had no wealth to steal. Slavers would hardly have approached a well-guarded place like the Priests' School; besides, at that time the Nuber polis were said to be keeping those vermin clear out of the Holy City.

I searched—into Penn, Conicut, Levannon, down to the southern extremity of our Empire, that pine-barren country. The clay image went with me, on the silver chain, in the box Sidney had made.

Sometimes, my lord, I dreamed the image might bring the Companion to me, even with word of Leopold. This was superstition, I admit. I cannot guess who made the image or with what ancient purpose, but when I contemplate either of the faces of enduring clay, the present drops from me, time is a murmur behind a curtain, I see my own breed as a blurred commotion in a stream wider and deeper than we suppose. A face of the image may say to me: *Why trouble with those who must soon be gone from the earth altogether in total sterility, or another plague year, or another thousand years of good intentions?* To this I find doubtful answers, and I dare to ask in return: *Why then has God made them? Or is God the Creator only one more fancy of this apelike nobody?* Then the image returns me stare for stare.

I am admitting, my Lord Abbot, that the image carried so long in boyhood by Leopold Graz can indeed stimulate heresy. But remember, I pray Your Beneficence will urge the Examiners to remember, Leopold was not carrying it when he went about as Brother Francis—I was. And though I have exposed my spirit to the clay, Your Beneficence knows I have lived in what we agree to call virtue. I think no one would whisper that I am in the grip of the Devil.

In 426 came the first rumor of an itinerant preacher calling himself Brother Francis. I was in Penn and southern Katskil early that year. Everyone expected some clash that would at last fire up the war against Moha. Emperor Mahonn was occupying his pinnacle of majesty at the Summer Palace of Lakurs, far from the Mohan border, uttering ambiguities. Diplomats, those well-fed errand boys, bounced from insult to insult, but Mohan travelers came to our country no more. And under this tension began those religious revivals, opening with prayer and shifting into orgies of hate. There might be a choir; the people would sing the fine hymns from the Third Century religious renascence—*In pace gaudeo* or *Exultate gentes*. Then preaching and praying, and soon enough the frenzied roaring: "*Down Moha! Destroy! Destroy!*"

According to the story rumor brought me, a slim man, very young, in a robe that some thought marked him as a lay brother of the Silvan Order, appeared at a meeting in the Stadium at Monsella and asked permission to speak, saying he was one Brother Francis, a messenger. When the Bishop of Solvan asked his place of origin, he replied: "My lord, who among us knows that?" The Bishop, moved by the power of his presence, permitted him to address the gathering. The voice of Brother Francis, rumor said, was not loud but so pure and moving that the people stood rock-quiet to hear him. Yet he was only describing a thing they knew intimately: the countryside between Nupal and the Mohan border city of Skoar.

He spoke of farms and villages they knew, of the Maypole dances, the churches where on Friday mornings they heard the words of Abraham explained. He talked of gardens, orchards, common things—the town greens and their pavilions; pastures near woods where the deer showed their proud heads in morning mist. He did not deny what they all knew, that poverty, cruelty, greed, and ignorance devour us; that human beings die from incomprehensible sickness or Old Time poison from the ground; that men are not altogether masters in the country of brown tiger and black wolf; that if our women escape sterility, at least one birth in every four is a mue. He denied no darkness, but he showed them their world as still a lovely thing. Then he told them in that same quiet voice: "If you follow the present direction of your lusts, the legions will walk here."

I suppose it was the voice and manner that moved them, for this argument has never yet deterred man from fouling his own nest. Some grumbled. One or two called, "God bless you!" Most were silent. When the Bishop sought their attention it was as though they could not quite catch the noise of him. They drifted away tranced, abandoning the Stadium to the Bishop and a few twittering officials. And Brother Francis—at this point rumor whispered excitedly—vanished. I suppose he stepped down to walk anonymously with the crowd.

Another tale reached me in May when I was returning to Kingstone. I discussed it with Sidney as we sat in his garden in the cloudy evening. "Miracles!" he said. "It was to be expected." Brother Francis had spoken at Grangorge, near the Moha border, and a man with a bent disordered spine, a cripple for years, tossed away his crutches and knelt to kiss the holy man's robe. Others were then and there healed of old afflictions. Sidney said: "The times are in a steamy state, Jermyn—it's this damned war, bound to come any minute. People have the need to believe. You notice the dear fella's preaching has no effect on the politicos. They hear only the noises of power."

"But here's power, if Brother Francis can sway a multitude."

"Yes, if." Sidney went on to speak of cures that baffled medical reason until one recognized the limited but amazing power of the mind over states of flesh. "I'd want to know how well that man walked the following day," he said, "but that's the part of the story we never get to hear. . . . I see you still wear Leo's amulet." We talked on about my brother, remembering loved qualities at random—his occasional stammer, his yen for fresh bread, his shyness with girls.

Leaving Kingstone in June, I fell in with some Ramblers whose Boss I knew. He told me of a meeting at Brakabin, where Brother Francis had said: "I speak of the City of Light."

Thus I knew. My Rambler friend could tell me nothing more. I hurried to Nuber, inquiring at the Abbey of the Silvan Order. They had been pestered by similar questions and were short with me: the man's robe was *not* that of a Silvan lay brother—it lacked the symbols; they knew and wished to know nothing of any Brother Francis. I went on to—never mind all that. Though frustrated for several more months, I did find him.

When the war began in September, 426, with the smashing of our garrison at the border town of Milburg, Katskil shivered at a prospect of Mohan columns driving south—down the Skoar River, through the hill passes, along the coast of the Hudson Sea. Had Moha tried this they might have won the war, but like our Empire, I daresay, they were ruled by the opaque stupidity of the military mind.

In those days of anxiety I caught word of a band of pilgrims who were marching up along the Delaware, intending to place themselves between the opposing armies in the no-man's-land that extended from Lake Skoar to the Hudson Sea, and these mad saints were led by Brother Francis. I hurried to Gilba, on the north shore of the lake, where they would pass if the story was true. I reached the town on a gleaming October afternoon, when the hills were purple under sunlight and rolling cloud shadows; but a section of the northern horizon was sullen with smoke—not forest fire, God knows, for the woods were soaked from recent rains. The pilgrims had arrived before me and were camped in a meadow at the edge of the town.

They were not saints but simple folk, some perhaps not even very religious, drawn by wonder at a truth-speaker. I have blamed Leopold for bringing them together in so vulnerable a crowd. Certainly his intention was to lead them between the opposing forces, armed only in their goodwill. And their innocent blood drenching the earth would have taught men what they have been taught through the millennia by the blood of other martyrs: namely, nothing.* In this I find the cruelty of the saint, who would have the devoted follow the dream—*his* dream, never understanding that it cannot be theirs for longer than the moment of enthusiasm. Since this particular massacre did not occur in the manner he may have foreseen, I suppose the question of Leopold's blame will be tossed about to the end of time, and no profit in it.

I asked a black-haired girl at the pilgrims' camp whether I might speak with Brother Francis. She said he was resting in his tent, but then she read my face, and in her kindness took me to him. My brother was asleep. Across eight years I knew him as though I had just then waked beside him in our old house on the Twenyet Road. At the girl's touch on his shoulder he came awake quickly—he always had—and asked: "Beata, my dear—is it time for prayers?"

"Not yet," she said, and I saw she loved him, not only as a believer loves a saint, but as a woman loves a man. "There's one here in need of you." Then she stared amazed from his face to mine, and presently left us.

I knelt by his cot, spoke his name, lost in the puzzled gaze of his so-familiar eyes. He said: "I'm sorry, sir—are you in trouble? What can I do for you? Why do you call me Leo?"

"Leopold, has your memory thrown me away?" For an instant I thought he was shaken, that he really knew me; then I could see in him only confusion. I recalled how once he had gashed

* *W.B. writes: "Can he expect the Church to condone this utterance?"*

his left arm in falling from a tree. "Here," I said, and shoved back the sleeve of his robe and found the scar, a jagged whiteness. "The oak near Rondo's Shrine—a hot August morning—I carried you to the shrine, where the priest bandaged and scolded you."

He searched my face, and told me he was sure I was not trying to deceive him; but was I not mistaken? "For my life began," he said, "in a nighttime room where I woke and knew I must go out into the world and learn the ways of it and become a messenger. I knew this from the Companion who spoke to me there, and came with me on my journey out of Nuber." He was speaking slowly, reminiscently, as if partly to himself. "I worked on farms. Sometimes I lived in the woods among the wild things. You see, I had never lived before—everything was new. I was held in a Moha prison once, for vagrancy. But before all this, you understand, I can't have been anything more than a germ of thought at the heart of chaos."

"Did you not change to your young man's form from a bony thirteen-year-old boy just into puberty, with a certain scar on his arm?"

He answered reasonably: "I suppose I did. Maybe there was a life before the one I know; some tell me there must have been. Forgive me if it's unkind—I can't pretend to remember you."

"Sidney Sturm? Jon Rohan?" I watched the beautiful saint's face, my anger not quite dying; maybe it *has* not quite died. "Louis Graz? Louis Graz and his wife, who died giving birth to a mue?"

"I am sorry, sir. Who were they?"

"Your father and mother, and mine. I am Jermyn Graz. I cared for you and loved you. I do now." I pulled the amulet from under my jacket. "You left this behind, Leo, in the dormitory of the Priests' School at Nuber eight years ago."

He opened the applewood box. Now, Sidney had made the fastening with such uncanny skill that it was quite concealed; no one could open it without a fumbling search unless he already knew the trick. Brother Francis opened it without hesitation. He looked on the clay image and said: "Oh, no! I could never have seen this before." He let the box drop, as if it hurt his fingers.

Outside the tent began a screaming uproar, and two soldiers of the Katskil Imperial Guard burst in, seizing my brother by the arms. "Are you he they call Brother Francis?"

"I am Brother Francis."

"Then I have a warrant for your arrest on a charge of treason against the sovereign people and the Emperor."

"I have done no treason."

"Not for us to judge. You are to come with us."

He made no resistance. His eyes warned me that any effort of mine to help would only worsen this new trouble. I have tried to imagine that his loss of memory was assumed to prevent my involvement in the disaster that he knew was about to overtake him; but no—those eyes were surely not seeing me as Jermyn Graz. Following in my stricken obscurity as the soldiers led him away, I saw how a platoon of the Guards was dispersing his followers with cudgels and whips, and gathering in some of them to be tied together like a string of slaves. The girl, that gentle Beata who had acted as my guide, flung herself at one of the men in a blind effort to reach Brother Francis, and was pushed to the ground. Her wrists were bound and she was carried off on a giant shoulder, unconscious, limp as a sack of meal.

As Your Beneficence knows, Brother Francis was taken to the military prison at Sofran and held there incommunicado for ten months. Through autumn and winter the war ground on. In April was fought the battle of Brakabin Meadows, and Jon Rohan, who had better have died there, wounded. Only after the war was over did I learn how another band of pilgrims had marched south from central Moha led by a disciple of Brother Francis, one Sister Adonaia. That group was intercepted in a mountain pass by Mohan soldiers, hunted down through the thickets, and butchered. As if, my lord, the two armies had agreed like feral lovers to sweep aside anything that threatened the consummation of their squalid embrace.

I will not try to tell of the trial. Let the Examiners study the transcript. Let them also consider the revulsion within the

Church itself after the war. Let them consider how the new Patriarch Benedict denounced the verdict against Brother Francis on many counts, saying that it was tainted by political expediency as well as bigotry—the Church had been hired, he said in effect, to do the hatchet work of an insane Emperor. (There does seem no doubt that the Emperor Mahonn was witless in the last year of his life, and that he was dressed in a wolfskin and drinking fresh chicken's blood when the assassins found him.) Let the Examiners consider how Patriarch Benedict invoked the Third Century ecclesiastical law *Contra Superbiam,* placing the whole Empire under a year's penance. Without this extreme reversal of the Church's position I could not have entered the monastic life.*

Sidney and I were refused admission to the Patriarchal Palace during the Preparatory Interrogations. We searched out Jon Rohan. How embittered he was—but he was drifting away from us even before the war. I told him of finding Leopold, of the refusal to admit us; we begged him to go in our place. A wounded veteran with the Iron Wheel of St. Franklin was less likely to be refused. But Jon would not believe Leopold could have become Brother Francis, whose very name Jon loathed. For some baffled words of mine defending the actions of Brother Francis, I thought poor distracted Jon would attack us with his crutch. His wife, disheartened, lovely Sara, begged us to go.

Then at Leopold's final trial and examination at the Lecture Hall of the Palace, I was admitted (but Sidney was not—perhaps they feared his wealth and distinction would weigh too heavily in the prisoner's favor) and the Archbishop of Orange permitted me to testify—what a mockery! Leopold, thin and haggard in his chains, denied me again; but not in quite the same way, my Lord Abbot. I felt he might be denying me for my own protection, lest I burn with him. Those judges were certainly determined to have his life. All but one perhaps: I read compassion in the face of one of them; but it was not a strong face, and he did not speak while I was there.

* *W.B. writes: "He convicts himself under* Contra Superbiam. *Who is he to judge the Church and speak as though it were subject to change?"*

Quickly the Archbishop's questioning led to the clay image. I was prepared for that trap. Seeing more clearly than I, Sidney had persuaded me to leave the image hidden at his house in Kingstone. If those judges connected Leopold to it, they would make of it idolatry, witchcraft, who knows what? I did badly, my lord—stammered, wept, disgraced myself. I denied knowledge of the image, was called a perjurer (as of course I was), dragged from the Hall, and searched. Sidney and I were banished from the Holy City.

And Jon did testify, that day. They must have held him in another anteroom, for we never saw him. He—

I will not write of that. It must be in the transcript.

Condemned, Leopold was taken to Kingstone. Behind a chain of polis and soldiers he was drawn in a slow cart to the stake in the marketplace. I was not the only one who called to him in love—if he could have heard it. I struggled to the edge of the crowd. A guard recognized me, secured me with an arm bent up behind my back, and grumbled at my ear: "Quiet, fool! We don't want to arrest you."

They lit the faggots at my brother's feet. The wood was damp; the smoke flung itself upward in a dirty cloud. I heard my brother cry out: "My Companion, have you forsaken me?" Moments later, above the priests' chanting, the flames, the rumbling of the storm that was reaching over the city, he called me. Very clearly I heard him call: "Jermyn, I have remembered you."

Fr. Jermyn, O.S.S., Precentor

§2

By Maeron of Nupal, Fr. Lit., Clericus Tribunalis Ecclesiae in the Patriarchate of Urbanus II: being a Digest of the Terminal Trial of the Heretic known as Brother Francis before the Court of Ecclesiastical Inquiry at Nuber, in the month of October in the Year of Abraham 427, His Grace the Archbishop of Orange Presiding Judge.

His Grace the Archbishop of Orange being present, the Court was opened on the 9th day of October, at or about the hour of Tierce, and before the judges was brought for final examination and judgment the prisoner calling himself Brother Francis and reputed by some to be one Leopold Graz son of the cobbler Louis Graz (deceased) of Twenyet Road in the City of Kingstone, this individual called Brother Francis being charged with heresy and certain related criminal actions as set forth in eight Articles.

Present on the dais were also the Most Reverend Jeffrey Sortees Lord Bishop of Nupal and, representing the Secular Estate, the Right Honorable Tomas Robson Earl of Cornal, Supervisor of the Ecclesiastical Prisons at Nuber.

The man called Brother Francis being present, the judge explained to the prisoner his rights at law, reminding him that during the Preparatory Interrogations he had refused the assistance of ecclesiastical counsel, and inquired whether he yet persisted in such refusal now that the matter had come to the point of final trial wherein he stood imperiled of his life.

The prisoner said he needed no defense but what he possessed.

His Grace said: Do you mean simply that you are in God's care?—but the Lord surely would have men aid one another in extremity.

The prisoner replied that he would not ask for counsel.

His Grace suggested that a defending counsel might aid that search for truth which was one of the major concerns of the trial. The prisoner replied that no other knew his heart, therefore no other should assume the burden of his defense.

Then, having been instructed concerning the sanctity of the oath, and that he ought to tell the truth as much for his soul's sake as out of respect for Church and Law, the prisoner said that he would tell the truth so far as he knew it, and so far as he was not forbidden to tell it by his conscience or by that Companion who to him was a second conscience and whose will he had accepted as a guide.

His Grace the Archbishop told him he could not make any

such reservations concerning the oath; and the Earl of Cornal also admonished him, saying that he was demanding a license to lie.

The prisoner said: Not so, my lord: I will not lie. But only God, if God lives, can command my mind; therefore I will not swear to tell everything, lest later I be forsworn.

His Grace asked: Do you doubt that God lives?

The man called Brother Francis said: Does any man live altogether without doubt, Your Grace? I have doubted it as one may doubt that the sun will rise.

His Grace said: It is perhaps a point of philosophy.

Bishop Sortees said: As for the reservation on the oath, Your Grace, is it not a reservation that any of us might make? If made out of true deference to the will of God I see no evil in it.

The Earl of Cornal said: But there is that matter of what he calls his Companion.

The prisoner then said that he would take the oath, but in no other way than he had stated, even if the torture were renewed and repeated until he died.

His Grace said: Well, let him be sworn to tell the truth as he understands it. I suppose no man can do more. We must not lose our way in irresponsible debate.

On these terms the prisoner willingly knelt, and having rested his forehead on the Book of Abraham, he made over his heart the sign of the Wheel and swore to tell the truth.

Then was read to the man called Brother Francis the First Article of the Charge.

ARTICLE I: *The man going by the name of Brother Francis is charged with making unproven claim to be a messenger of God.*

Questioned as to the truth of this, the prisoner said: I do not claim and have never claimed it.

His Grace said: But you have called yourself a messenger?

The prisoner said: I have, but cannot tell who sent me.

His Grace asked: Cannot, or will not, my son?

The prisoner said: I cannot, Your Grace. I do not know.

Earl Robson said: It might have been the Devil?

The prisoner said: I have never had reason to think so.

Reminded by His Grace that some of his followers had declared under the ordeal that they believed him to be sent by God, the prisoner said they must have spoken whatever their hearts believed, but not what they knew, since he did not know it himself.

Earl Robson of Cornal said: I can't understand this, a man who carries a message, or thinks he does, not knowing who sent him.

The prisoner said: But for the direction of my Companion, I would not call myself a messenger; and my Companion may well be of the chosen of God. I think he is; but he has not told me so.

The Earl of Cornal then remarked that, with deference to his colleagues of the Ecclesia, he considered the prisoner had already convicted himself under the First Article of the Charge. His Grace requested the view of the Lord Bishop of Nupal, who said that while he felt the prisoner had so far spoken with reason and humility, he would not further commit himself at this moment.

Then was read to the prisoner the Second Article of the Charge.

ARTICLE II: *The man going by the name of Brother Francis is charged with accepting guidance in all his actions from a being outside the common perceptions of men, whom he calls his Companion, in defiance of the First Law of Holy Church as laid down in the Book of Abraham, Chapter Five, Section Seven: THOU SHALT SET NO AUTHORITY ABOVE THE AUTHORITY OF ALMIGHTY GOD AS DEFINED BY HIS ANOINTED.*

Questioned as to the truth of the charge, the prisoner stated that he had accepted the guidance of his Companion in all actions, but only in the manner in which others might accept the guidance of priests, believing that their counsel would not be contrary to God's will so far as any human being can know it.

His Grace said: But you have no reason except your own opinion, the feeling of your own heart, to believe that this Companion can be regarded as one of God's anointed?

After reflection the prisoner said: No, Your Grace: it is true that I have formed this belief in the light of my own opinion and conscience.

His Grace said: You will admit, then, that unless it can be proved that your Companion is one of God's anointed, you stand convicted of heresy under the Second Article?

The prisoner said: I can hardly deny it.

Bishop Sortees asked: But you have sincerely believed that your Companion would require nothing of you that violated God's laws?

The prisoner said: Yes, Father, I believe that.

The Earl of Cornal inquiring whether the prisoner had known his Companion by any other name, the prisoner denied it. Asked by the Earl to describe the Companion, the prisoner said he had seen him only with the eyes of his mind.

The Earl of Cornal said: You are unreasonable. You are attempting to confuse the Court with metaphysics.

The prisoner said: My lord, I use what words I find. I know my Companion; I do not see him as I see your lordship in the flesh.

His Grace the judge asked: Is he with you now, my son?

The prisoner said: No, Your Grace.

His Grace asked: Is it long since he has been with you?

The prisoner said: It has been long. He has not been with me since the day of my arrest.

His Grace asked: Never during the Preparatory Interrogations? He was not with you on the day when, because of contumacious refusals, it was necessary for you to undergo physical persuasion?

The prisoner said: Had he been with me then, Your Grace, I could have borne the torture with a better heart.

His Grace asked: Do you draw any conclusion from this absence of your Companion while you have been in the custody of the Church?

The prisoner said: I draw no conclusion, Your Grace. I remember too well that in the ten months of my imprisonment in the military prison at Sofran, when I was accused of treason but not of heresy, my Companion was not with me.

His Grace asked: Do you think it possible then that your

Companion may have been only the substance of an illusion which has now passed from you? You must know, my son, that the Church has no wish to punish anyone for a malady of the mind.

The prisoner replied quickly and firmly that his Companion was no illusion.

Then the Earl of Cornal asked: Have you ever accompanied your Companion to certain meetings?

The man called Brother Francis said: He was often with me when I spoke to the people, to those who joined my company.

Earl Robson said: That is not the question. Have you ever gone, with this being you call a Companion, to meetings of any group called a coven, a meeting of those who deny the divinity of our Savior Abraham and of his prophet of Old Time Jesus Christ?

The prisoner said: No.

The Earl said: You will answer with respect.

The prisoner said: I know nothing of witchcraft, my lord, but I believe it to be a delusion.

The Earl said: Your Grace, is not that heresy in itself?

His Grace the Archbishop replied that the entire question of witchcraft was a matter of dispute, and that no doubt much light would be shed on it in the next Council on the Creed. He suggested also that with regard to this prisoner, this line of inquiry had apparently been exhausted, and with negative result, in the Preparatory Interrogations, and during the physical persuasion that the Earl himself had attended as Supervisor of the Prisons. His Grace then asked the prisoner: If your Companion should come to you while you are on trial here, will you know it?

The prisoner said: I will know it, Your Grace.

His Grace asked: And will you tell us of it?

The prisoner said: If my Companion permits it.

His Grace said: Have a care, my son, how you set the whim of this unknown Companion above the authority of the Ecclesia.

The prisoner said: I have already stated that I have obeyed all the directions of my Companion, even against my will.

The Lord Bishop of Nupal asked him: But if your Companion required you to perform some act forbidden by the laws of

God, you would not perform it, would you?

The prisoner said: Father, I think this could not happen.

His Grace said: But you must answer the Lord Bishop's question, and do so remembering your oath.

The prisoner said: I think the will and the laws of God have always been explained by some human agency, and these are fallible.

His Grace said: My son, Bishop Sortees' most kindly worded question deserved no such response, which we find over the borderline of heresy. If you continue headstrong and impudent, you will compel us to find you guilty under the Second Article.

Then was read to the prisoner the Third Article of the Charge.

ARTICLE III: *The man going by the name Brother Francis is charged with claiming to have begun life miraculously, without father or mother, in the body of a boy about thirteen years of age.*

In response to the reading of this Charge, the prisoner declared that he had claimed no miracle but merely described what had happened to the best of his knowledge: that his conscious life had indeed commenced at that apparent age, with no memory of an earlier existence.

The Lord Bishop of Nupal said: But this would be a miracle, astonishing as a virgin birth. No childhood?

His Grace reminded Bishop Sortees that cases of lost memory were not unknown, a malady of the mind that was very possibly a punishment for secret sins, and thus no miracle was necessarily involved.

The man called Brother Francis said: I think this may be, Your Grace. God may have taken my memory, but perhaps to strengthen me as a messenger, or for other reasons that I cannot know. I do know that I woke as if from a void: I was; and my Companion guided me.

Bishop Sortees said: I am amazed. I should have taken time to read the record of the Preparatory Interrogations. You woke, Brother Francis, knowing the speech of men?

The Earl of Cornal remarked it had been agreed that the

prisoner was not to be addressed as "Brother" since he had demonstrated no right to the title, as would be stated in the Fourth Article. Bishop Sortees apologized for his error, reminding the Earl that he had come uninstructed to the Court in the place of the Bishop of Ulsta, who was ill. Then he repeated his question to the prisoner.

The prisoner said: I must have done so, Father, since my Companion spoke to me and I understood him.

The Lord Bishop asked: And no childhood, my son? No childhood?

The prisoner said: I cannot remember any, Father.

The Earl asked: Well, what kind of voice has your Companion?

The prisoner said he knew that voice with the hearing of his mind.

Earl Robson said: Oh, again, again! Metaphysics!

His Grace the Archbishop then spoke of delusions wherein the deluded may be innocent of evil intent; and the Bishop of Nupal declared that he thought the prisoner spoke with no evil intent but rather like one impelled by a dream; and His Grace warned against premature judgments before completion of the reading of the Articles.

The Earl of Cornal said: But I ask myself, Your Grace, what motive the accused can have had for claiming this miraculous or seemingly miraculous thing, other than a wish to dazzle his befuddled followers.

His Grace said: Let us continue.

Then was read to the prisoner the Fourth Article of the Charge.

ARTICLE IV: *The man going by the name Brother Francis is charged with unlawfully assuming that title, being not a member of any religious body recognized by the Holy Murcan Church, and with wearing a robe simulating that of a lay brother of the Ordo Sancti Silvani.*

In response to this charge the prisoner stated that when he woke to life it was with the knowledge of the Companion calling him, and by the name Brother Francis; that the Companion had always called him by this name and no other, and that he could not remember responding to any other name. As for the robe, he declared it had been made for him by a woman of his company who knew nothing of religious orders. He also respectfully inquired whether there was an actual law of Church or State that forbade a man to call himself Brother or allow himself to be so addressed if he was not a member of a religious order.

The Earl of Cornal said: Verily the Devil is a lawyer. Everyone knows the title is proper only to a monk. Statute or no statute, can this fellow require us to overlook the tradition of the ages to suit his whim? And how should a woman make a monk's robe not knowing what she did?

His Grace said: My lord of Cornal, we must not assume too much. This may even be a case of true ignorance on both counts. The prisoner's robe, I remind you, did not carry the symbol of the Wheel, nor the symbol of crossed shovels that defines a lay brother's status. And to the prisoner His Grace said: We must warn you, however, that by accepting "Brother" as a title you have caused in some persons a mistaken notion that you spoke with the authority of the Church. This was at least a deception, whether or not by intent.

The prisoner said: Your Grace, I admit my error in this. I told those who joined me that I was no churchman; I ought to have told them not to address me in a way that could cause misunderstanding.

Earl Robson said: Your Grace, I think he buys a great sin with a small penance.

His Grace said: My son, you have spoken with humility, yet I feel a defiance in you still. Are you defiant, at heart?

After long silence, during which His Grace desired that the accused be not interrupted but given time to reflect and consult his conscience, the man calling himself Brother Francis replied: No, Your Grace, I do not think I am.

Bishop Sortees of Nupal asked: In accepting the title "Brother" were you perhaps intending to implement that ancient wish for the brotherhood of man which our Savior Abraham declared in the words: "Let us be born again together"—could this be?

The prisoner said: Those are words that I treasure, Father, but I can say no more than I have said. I woke, and my Companion called me by that name.

Then was read to the prisoner the Fifth Article of the Charge.

ARTICLE V: *The man going by the name Brother Francis is charged with speaking against the sacrament of marriage, has lived in open sin with a common harlot, and has inspired the women of his company with such a concupiscent hysteria that they believe him to be a god.*

Questioned as to this, the prisoner replied that he had once said, to those friends who marched with him to the meadow of Gilba, that he did not suppose marriage was the only good way men and women might live together. He said he did not think this amounted to speaking against a sacrament. As for the remainder of the charge, he said it was absurd.

The Earl of Cornal asked: Do you deny then that you lived in carnal intimacy, while going about under the name Brother Francis, with one Beata Firmin, a common prostitute?

The prisoner said: Beata Firmin was caught up in the life of a prostitute at an earlier time; she had abandoned it before joining our company. If it has a bearing on my trial for heresy, I do not deny that I loved her, but my Companion has commanded me to live chastely for the sake of my mission. Often Beata slept in my tent, but we had no carnal knowledge of each other.

Earl Robson said: More fool you, she's a handsome woman.

The man calling himself Brother Francis said: Well, my lord, you cannot accuse me both of fornication and of the avoidance of it.

Earl Robson said: Nay then, nay, we must cease jesting. I remind you that you are on trial for criminal actions as well as for heresy.

The prisoner said: I cannot conceive how my friendship for Beata Firmin can be described as a criminal action.

Bishop Sortees said: My lord, surely any criminal actions, to be judged by this Court, must bear a relation to the charge of heresy.

The Earl said: Your Reverence, I think the relation can be shown. And to the prisoner he said: You are aware that the woman Beata Firmin believes you to be a god?

The prisoner said: I have been separated from her for ten months. Ten months ago I am certain she had no such delusion.

The Earl said: Why, man, she speaks of nothing but you and your divinity. She rants, she drivels, she bites her lips to make them red and pleasing against the dream of your return, she sits in her cell with a pillow under her smock and croons to it, saying she is with child by the Divine Brother and the child's dear name shall be Jesus. Is the Companion with you now?

The prisoner replied: My Lord Robson, if your prison has brought Beata Firmin to this state, I will pray God to forgive you in Hell, since it is beyond my human power to forgive.

His Grace said: Finish the reading of the Articles.

The Earl said: It seems I have been cursed by a witch.

His Grace said to him: My lord, my lord, no more jesting. Finish the reading, Clerk.

But Earl Robson of Cornal said: Your Grace, as God is my witness I am not jesting. The moment after this prisoner cursed me I was taken with a violent pain in my right hand.

Bishop Sortees said: But he did not curse your lordship. He said he would pray for your forgiveness by the Almighty, and had I spoken as you did, I declare to you I would feel need of such forgiveness myself.

His Grace asked: Do you wish an adjournment, my lord of Cornal, or may we continue with the reading of the Articles?

The Earl of Cornal said: I ask no adjournment, Your Grace. I will bear it. But I wish this fellow to know, I say to him in open court, if he slips off our griddle here in the Court of the Ecclesia, I'll fetch him down with a charge of witchcraft under secular law, and it shall go hard with him.

Then was read to the prisoner the Sixth Article of the Charge.

ARTICLE VI: *The man going by the name Brother Francis is charged with professing to heal the sick by miraculous means.*

In response to this the prisoner said that he professed nothing except his message; that some persons might have found healing in his presence, at times when the Companion was with him, and that if God had truly healed them it must have been done by his Companion rather than by himself.

The Earl of Cornal said: And your Companion, we understand, politely declines to be questioned by this Court?

The prisoner said: My Companion is not here.

The Earl said: A pity, a pity. I should admire to ask his opinion concerning the pain in my hand.

The man known as Brother Francis did not answer. Then was read to him the Seventh Article of the Charge.

ARTICLE VII: *The man going by the name Brother Francis is charged with wantonly leading a band of his followers to a place of peril between the savage invading host of Moha and the defenders of the Empire.*

His Grace the Archbishop said: Since the fact itself is not in dispute, I will only ask how you explain this action.

The prisoner said: We hoped to illuminate the nature of war.

His Grace said: You must know the Church is deeply opposed to war. Why did you not work through the Church?

The prisoner said: That month, Your Grace, Masses were being said for the victory of the Imperial arms.

His Grace replied: Naturally. Since the Holy City is located within the Empire, an attack on Katskil is an attack on Holy Church; therefore the rights of the case are not in question. In any event, your followers were merely swept aside, as you must have known they would be. Why this empty gesture? You placed your people between fire and fire without a shield. Had the Guard not intervened and dispersed them, many lives might have been lost.

The prisoner said: I hear that many of my company were arrested, some questioned under torture, none released except by death.

His Grace explained that this was a political and military problem, not within the competence of the Ecclesiastical Court. The prisoner then stood silent a long time, and appeared like one listening, and there was whispering among the members of the Ecclesia privileged to attend as spectators, which His Grace the Judge was obliged to silence, the prisoner seeming unaware of this. At length the prisoner said: Your Grace, we sought to illuminate the nature of war. But I understand now that the greatest evil is not war itself but the love of war. However, Your Grace, is it not a fact that the armies did not meet that day?

His Grace said: What reasoning is this? They met later, and at that very place. Did you not hear in prison about the battle of Gilba?—I am told that Mohan forces still hold the highlands north of the lake. So what price your intervention? And the armies met at Brakabin Meadows in the following spring, another disaster. There is a witness to be called who was wounded at Brakabin. You shall see for yourself, sir, how effectively your dangerous dream has prevented war. Well?

The prisoner said: Your Grace, we never had great hope of preventing the continuation of this war; only, as I have said, to illuminate the nature of war. In any case, I did as my Companion directed me, and I would do the same again.

Earl Robson said: But maybe with fewer followers?

The man called Brother Francis replied: Maybe with a million followers. Or with two or three. I would do the same again.

His Grace then gently asked the prisoner whether he had been listening a moment past to his Companion, and the prisoner replied: I cannot answer that, Your Grace, because I am not certain.

The Bishop of Nupal said: Your Grace, I have read of some in Old Time who went up unarmed against the machineries of war. Certain priests and others burned their own bodies in protest at evils they found intolerable. It is folly perhaps; but so far I can find no sin in this man.

His Grace said: It is true this Article deals with a social and military issue. However, the wisdom of the Court has included it among the charges of heresy, and so we must consider it.

Earl Robson said: Does it not seem, Your Grace, that this prisoner has set himself up to judge between the nations as only God can judge? The issues of the battlefield, surely, are decided by God and God alone, not by fanatic preachers.

His Grace said: This will be weighed, my lord of Cornal. Does your hand still pain you?

The Earl replied: There is only one more Article to read. After that, if Your Grace thinks best, we might adjourn till tomorrow.

Then was read to the prisoner the Eighth Article of the Charge.

ARTICLE VIII: *The man going by the name Brother Francis is charged with deluding his followers by talk of a coming heaven on earth described as a City of Light, in contravention of Holy Doctrine as set forth in the Book of Abraham, Chapter Five, Section Seven: THOU SHALT CHERISH NO TREASURE ON EARTH OR IN THE THOUGHT OF EARTH, WHICH IS SOON TO PERISH AND PASS AWAY.*

In reply to this, the prisoner said that he had never described the City of Light as a heaven on earth, or ever intentionally deluded anyone in any way.

His Grace asked him: What then is the City of Light?

The man called Brother Francis said: In the City of Light no violence is done to the body of earth or to the human body or spirit. The light of the City is the light of understanding and love, the two inseparable.

His Grace asked: It is a dream of earth and not of Heaven?

The man called Brother Francis said: It is not a dream of Heaven on earth, for in the City of Light men may strive for perfection, I suppose, but they do not reject the good that is attainable.

His Grace said: And for this dream of earth you have endured imprisonment and physical persuasion, and may suffer worse: was this not for the sake of persuading others to share your dream, and leave their appropriate labors, and follow you?

The man called Brother Francis replied: I do not urge or persuade. I tell the vision as I see it, and I think those who followed me were sharing it for at least a part of my journey.

His Grace said: As far as the meadow at Gilba, where the armies might have rolled over them. My son, there have been visionaries before who perverted the just course of life. Do you not see the result when men turn aside from their necessary labors after a moon-blink, an *ignis fatuus?* Who shall plow and sow, and tend the fields, and mind the harvest? You must have been taught, perhaps in the childhood you do not remember, how God has placed us on this miserable earth for a time of trial, so that souls deserving of Heaven may be winnowed out from the unworthy, and how then the earth shall pass away and be as a drop of water in the firmament. Do you not see, my son, that no other explanation of our presence here is possible, since we must believe that God is all-loving and all-powerful? Why do we concern ourselves with heresy at all, if not to protect our people from straying into disaster? To dazzle the credulous with your vision of a City of Light on earth is to betray them, to hide from them this truth that God's revelation through Abraham has made clear to us. And whether your heart's intent is evil or benevolent, the result is the same as though the Devil himself had stood at your shoulder and charmed the gullible with your voice.

The man called Brother Francis replied: Yet there is a City of Light. I said to those who followed and heard me: There is a battle of Armageddon, where good and evil confront each other for a decision, not for all time but for the time that you know; and there is a City of Light on earth, built by your labor not for all time but for the time that you know. Every day, every night the battle of Armageddon is to be fought, and won or lost: see that you find courage. Every night, every day something is given to the building of the City of Light or taken from it: see that your share is given, and with goodwill. The battle is within you; the city is for all your kind, not for all time but for the time that you know.

At this hour the session of examination and judgment was adjourned until morning of the following day.

His Grace the Archbishop of Orange being present, the Court was opened on the 10th day of October, at or about the hour of Tierce, for the second day of the final judgment and examination in the case of the prisoner charged with heresy who calls himself Brother Francis.

Present as before were the Most Reverend Jeffrey Sortees Lord Bishop of Nupal, and the Rt. Hon. Tomas Robson Earl of Cornal, who attended this session with his right hand covered by a bandage. His Grace the Archbishop graciously inquired whether his lordship was still in pain; the Earl replied he would willingly bear it rather than delay the trial, adding that all those present yesterday must bear in mind that they were witnesses to what had occurred.

The prisoner being then brought to the dock and chained, His Grace announced that one Jermyn Graz, itinerant cobbler of no known address, had urged his right to testify before the Court, and that this request had been granted. Master Graz came forward and was sworn.

To him His Grace said: When you demanded admission to the Preparatory Interrogations it was denied, Master Graz, in view of the improbability of your story and the fact that the accused disavowed any knowledge of your name. Since then other information has come to us tending to support your claim to be heard. You are sworn; I must further caution you to limit yourself to the questions put to you. I request you to look now on the accused and say whether you know him.

Master Graz looked on the prisoner and said: He is my brother, Your Grace. He is my beloved brother.

His Grace then directed the accused to look on the cobbler Jermyn Graz and say whether he knew him.

The prisoner said: I know him as the man who came to my tent at Gilba on the day I was arrested. If I ever saw him before then, the memory is gone with all my other memories of childhood.

Master Graz said: He is my brother. He disappeared from the

Priests' School at Nuber in 418. It was the 7th of December.

His Grace said: Master Graz, when we learned something of this from another source, we spoke to the Headmaster of the Priests' School. The records do show that a boy Leopold Graz, thirteen (your brother we do not doubt), did vanish that day. But the Headmaster Father Ricordi was shown the man called Brother Francis at the prison, and would not say with any certainty that he was Leopold Graz, and you have now heard the prisoner testify that he does not know you. Then His Grace asked the accused: Have you any recollection of attending the Priests' School at Nuber, or any school?

The prisoner said: I have none, Your Grace.

His Grace said: But when Father Ricordi described to you the Senior Dormitory at the school as it would look by candlelight, you remembered this as the place where you had, as you say, waked to life?

The prisoner said: That is true, Your Grace.

Master Graz said: He is my brother.

An attending officer of the Court was then obliged to restrain the witness from climbing the barrier into the dock; the man was weeping and appeared beside himself. Being restrained, he apologized to the Court for his behavior.

His Grace said: Subject to your dissent, my lords, I think we may accept the probability that the man called Brother Francis is indeed Leopold Graz, once of Kingstone, who has suffered the loss of memory of his childhood, under what divine punishment we know not. There being no dissent, His Grace said further: We have then an identity for the prisoner, and will address him from now on as Leopold Graz. But I point out to you that this does not further our inquiry, unless the history of his childhood produces evidence bearing on the charge of heresy. I will ask you now, Master Graz, if you have recovered control of yourself, whether you are acquainted with a Captain Jon Rohan.

Master Graz said: I am, Your Grace, or I was. We were boys together, Jon and another friend and my brother Leopold and I.

His Grace asked: Have you seen Captain Rohan recently?

Master Graz said: Not for a month or more. I went to see him when I was refused admission to the Preparatory Interrogations, hoping he might be allowed to testify in my place. He told me he believed my brother was dead. As a soldier he hated and despised Brother Francis from what he had heard about him, and refused to consider that Brother Francis might be Leopold. Jon still suffers from an unhealed wound. He was not himself; I should have forgiven it. We parted in anger.

His Grace said: We have spoken with him, rather our representatives have, and with your other friend Dr. Sturm. You yourself are better known to us than you may suppose. What can you tell us concerning a clay image once in the possession of your brother Leopold?

Master Graz then appeared startled and confused, stammering and saying he knew of no image belonging to his brother.

The Earl of Cornal said: You are under oath, Master Graz.

Master Graz said: Ah, you mean *my* little amulet. I had one till lately, the sort I'm sure the Church hasn't disapproved. But my brother would never have cared for anything like that. He was always deeply religious, Your Grace. He would have found it sacrilegious.

His Grace asked: This idol is not now in your possession?

Master Graz replied: No, Your Grace. I lost it some time back.

The Bishop of Nupal would then have questioned him, but His Grace intervened, saying: My lord, whether or not he is lying about possession of the image, he has perjured himself on another count, as testimony that follows will show, and we cannot permit the Court of the Ecclesia to be contaminated by a perjurer. Attendant, take this man Jermyn Graz to the anteroom, strip him, and search him for the possession of any sort of charm or amulet. If any is found, he is to be committed to the prison for examination. If not, he is to be conducted to the border of the Holy City of Nuber and warned not to return within a year, and he is to consider himself fortunate in the leniency of this Court. Master Graz was removed, and His Grace addressed the prisoner: Leopold Graz, I note that you have become very white. Do you wish the help of a physician?

The prisoner said: No, Your Grace, a physician cannot help me.

His Grace asked: You do admit, then, that you may stand in need of help for your soul's sake? And when the prisoner appeared unable to answer, His Grace gently inquired: For your soul's sake, what can you tell us concerning a clay image, male and female, in a box of applewood fastened to a silver chain?

After much hesitation, the prisoner said: Your Grace, I have no knowledge of any such thing.

The Earl of Cornal said: Have you lost your memory for recent events also? Did not that man Jermyn Graz show you such an image in your tent at Gilba?

The prisoner said: No, my lord. No.

His Grace then called Captain Jon Rohan, who came from the west anteroom with the assistance of an attendant, and was sworn. His Grace asked: Captain Rohan, you are a veteran of the battle of Brakabin Meadows, wounded in the service of His Majesty the Emperor?

The witness replied: I am, Your Grace.

His Grace asked: You testify here willingly, under no duress, Captain Rohan, and in accordance with our previous conversations at the time you volunteered to appear before this Court?

The witness replied: I do, Your Grace.

His Grace said: I will ask whether in former years you were acquainted with a boy named Leopold Graz, son of the cobbler Louis Graz of Twenyet Road in Kingstone?

The witness said: I was, Your Grace. He was five years younger than I, and I was a playmate of his elder brother when he was born. I knew him until his thirteenth year, when he disappeared from the Priests' School at Kingstone.

His Grace said: Look on the accused, Captain Rohan, and say whether you know him.

Captain Rohan looked long on the man called Brother Francis and said: Yes, that is Leopold Graz, though greatly changed.

His Grace then directed the prisoner to look on Captain

Rohan well and say whether he knew him. The prisoner said with apparent indifference: He is quite unknown to me.

Captain Rohan said: He knows me. He has betrayed his country and his people. He cannot hide behind mystery. He knows, Your Grace, he knows I understand him.

Bishop Sortees said: You are not here to judge, Captain Rohan. I pray Your Grace will instruct him to limit himself to the question.

His Grace said: You must do that, Captain Rohan. I ask you now to tell what you know of the childhood of Leopold Graz.

Captain Rohan said: He possessed great charm, as a boy, but he was what people call fey. Strange, ungovernable, given to outrageous fancies. He became fascinated by an obscene clay image, an object indecently representing both sexes in one body, that his brother secured for him from a Gypsy when Leopold was about seven, and which I think was never out of Leopold's possession until he disappeared from the Priests' School.

His Grace asked: And this obsession with a clay image, was it associated with any other thing that you recall as unusual?

Captain Rohan testified: It was, Your Grace. Very soon after his brother gave him the image, Leopold was speaking of an invisible companion who gave him guidance.

The Lord Bishop of Nupal said: Captain Rohan, is this not quite a common thing in childhood? A child, especially a lonely one, is often given to such fancies, surely.

Captain Rohan said: But this did not pass away as we expect childhood fancies to do, Your Reverence. Yes, my own little daughter chattered of such a thing once, and I corrected her, and soon heard no more about it. But this boy Leopold continued to believe in his spectral companion—and does so still, I understand. We others, being ignorant boys, were much impressed by his talk, and I am sorry to say we encouraged it awhile. I stopped doing so when I realized that it bordered on idolatry, or perhaps passed the border.

The Earl of Cornal asked: Do you say that he in fact worshiped this idol, this image?

Captain Rohan testified: My lord, he would hold it in his hands, and often close his eyes and appear to be listening; and then he might give us advice on matters of which he could have known nothing. It was, I remember, advice much more mature than belonged to his years.

His Grace asked: And what, if you know, became of this clay image?

Captain Rohan said: The boy Leopold left it behind when he disappeared from the Priests' School. I believe Sidney Sturm brought it back to Leopold's brother Jermyn, and it was still in Jermyn's possession a month ago when he and Dr. Sturm came to see me.

His Grace said: Leopold Graz, under oath before God to tell the truth, do you say you do not know this man Captain Rohan?

The prisoner said: I know his nature from the way he speaks.

His Grace said: You evade. Do you remember him from the past?

The prisoner said: I cannot answer that.

His Grace said: What? You cannot?

The prisoner said: I took the oath with reservations of which I made no secret. I cannot answer the question.

His Grace said: And you deny any knowledge of a clay image?

After hesitation, the prisoner replied: I do.

His Grace asked: This you say under oath? . . . Leopold Graz, you must speak so that we hear you, and stand upright if you are able. You declare under oath that you know nothing of any clay image?

The man Leopold Graz called Brother Francis said: The light of the City is the light of understanding and love, the two inseparable.

His Grace the Archbishop then said: There need be no more testimony, no more questioning. The rest, my lords, is for discussion among us three, *in camera*. We insist that there be no loose discussion of this troublesome case by those privileged to attend this hearing as spectators. The Court is now adjourned.

Final judgment and sentence will be pronounced on the opening of this Court tomorrow.

§3

Letter from Mgr. Wilmot Breen, Magister Theologiae, *Director of Examiners under the Patriarchate of Pretorius IV, to His Beneficence Alesandar Fitzeral, O.S.S., Abbot of St. Benjamin's at Mount Orlook, November 29, 465.*

To Your Beneficence, Greetings.

Speedily and with the help of God we have reached a decision in the question of the blessed Francis of Gilba, and have communicated our finding to His Holiness Pretorius IV by the Will of Heaven Patriarch of the World. It is now our great pleasure to convey to Your Beneficence also the substance of our findings, with gratitude for the assistance so graciously granted us by Your Beneficence in securing the document by Jermyn Graz, which in spite of its dubious nature sheds much light on the childhood of the blessed Francis.

We find that beyond doubt Francis of Gilba was divinely inspired in his teaching (so unfortunately never committed to writing) and that in particular his insistence on truthfulness, divine understanding, and divine love as the essence of the everlasting Brownist Faith is a great contribution toward the salvation of mankind. We feel confident that when sufficient time has passed, this noble spirit will be declared sanctified. In the meantime Your Beneficence will be pleased to learn that the arm bone of the blessed Francis preserved at the Cathedral in Albani continues its work of healing to the manifest glory of God.

We have found that the Companion who appeared to the blessed Francis in his visions was no other than the blessed St. Lucy of Syracuse, martyred in ancient time and venerated throughout the centuries. Understanding in this matter was granted to us in a dream, wherein it was made plain that in speaking of the City of Light, Francis of Gilba was approaching as nearly as God permitted him to explaining the identity of his sacred benefactress: LUCY from ancient Latin LUX, meaning LIGHT. After this guidance it was a simple matter to consult the records, wherein we found that Francis of Gilba, vulgarly known as Leopold Graz, was born on December 13, St. Lucy's Day since time immemorial. Thus all doubt was dispelled: the dross of argument and conjecture fell away and the intention of the Lord was made plain.

We find further, having questioned the benign and ancient woman Mam Lora Stone at the nunnery of St. Ellen at Nupal, that the birth of Francis of Gilba must have been miraculous. St. Lucy, be it remembered, is a patron of women in childbirth. We need not presume any event so marvelous as a virgin birth, but simply that the mother of Francis was gotten with child by an angelic visitation. A clue to this is unwittingly provided in the manuscript by the man Jermyn Graz, in the passage recording the obscure saying of the boy Francis that he was "born unto the Vine." The Vine, as we know, is sacred to the Archangel Dionysus, the Male Principle, and now that the identity of the Companion is known, the conclusion is obvious.

This brings us to a delicate matter wherein we must rely on the discretion of Your Beneficence. The manuscript of the man Jermyn Graz, which we had hoped to return for the archives of St. Benjamin's, has disappeared, owing, we believe, to the criminal dereliction of some minor member of our clerical staff; all of them are to be put to the question, and no doubt the truth will emerge. In the meantime, by the grace of God, a fair copy of the manuscript had been made, from which the gross errors and perversions of the man Jermyn Graz were eliminated; thus we now have a record that is reliable for all time, and if the original manuscript should be recovered, it will probably be the consensus of the Examiners that it ought to be destroyed, not preserved.

The miraculous generation of the blessed Francis of Gilba is rendered even more clear by the fact that Francis could not logically have been whole brother to this man who for many years has been precentor at St. Benjamin's, and who appears to have wormed his way into the affections of Your Beneficence, and whose opinions as they appear in the uncorrected manuscript are tainted with gross heresy and sinful pride and willful error. Your Beneficence will understand that this man Jermyn Graz must be instantly removed from any position at the Abbey, and held in close custody until the Examiners shall have had opportunity to study his literary output—collected stories, legends, commentaries on Old Time, we know not what—and determine whether to place them on the Index Expurgatorius and burn all copies.

Finally—and this is a matter of the utmost urgency—any amulet or image or the like found in the possession of the man Jermyn Graz is to be confiscated and turned over to us for exorcism and disposal. If no such object is found in his possession, he must be persuaded by any approved means to explain his disposition of it. The blessed Francis of Gilba himself repudiated this miserable idol with horror; other implications, we feel sure, will not escape the consideration of Your Beneficence.

Accept, we pray, the assurance of our continual esteem.

Wilmot Breen, M.T.

§4

Note from unfrocked prisoner Jermyn Graz to His Beneficence Alesandar Fitzeral, O.S.S., Abbot of St. Benjamin's.

My dear Lord Abbot:

Pray accept my gratitude for the kindness of Your Beneficence in transferring me to this cell where an eastern window permits me a little morning light, and for allowing me these writing materials, and for permitting me to make this communication to Your Beneficence.

I will first take this opportunity to recant whatever confession of error I may have made under physical persuasion, and second, to repeat as clearly as I can that which I said to my examiners and which they would not accept, concerning my disposal of the two-faced clay.

After I had committed to the hands of Your Beneficence my Memorandum on the life of my brother Leopold, reflection made it clear to me that the discovery of the image on my person, considering the present temper of the times, might result in peril to the clay figure as well as to myself. I remind Your Beneficence that I have been and still am a historian. To me, in this ugly little dab of clay, there is a beauty and a wonder that I cannot describe to you: these faces have seen eternity. Why it was rejected by my poor brother, if indeed it was, I shall never know; but I cannot repudiate it: these faces that have seen eternity are the faces of my own kind.

Therefore on leaving Your Beneficence I took myself for a long walk into the woods outside the monastery grounds, or perhaps beyond the woods, and I buried the image. It is in the applewood box that my beloved Sidney made for it, the silver chain is wrapped around it, and it lies in a place where it will not be found by any search—for even I, having smoothed the natural cover and moved away heeding no landmarks, could not find it again if I would. The Examiners and their servants cannot overturn all the trees and boulders or dig away all the earth in all the places where I might have buried it.

Let it lie there and be discovered again—maybe by a child, or a poet, or a wanderer, in a time when the passions of our day are no more remembered than those of Old Time.

Jermyn Graz

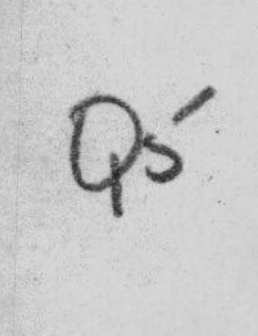